The Haunting of Alice

Books by R.H.Matthews

The Spirit of the Willow

The Haunting Of Alice

Rossalyn H Matthews

The Haunting of Alice

2020

In memory of Michael

With thanks to Lisa for her patience and
understanding

THE BEGINNING.

I stood at the window watching the dark winter clouds roll over the sea, I saw the first flakes of snow fall from the laden sky. Far down on the shoreline I could see some sort of movement, in the dim light I could just make out the silhouettes of a group of men, they held flaming torches, odd I thought, it was such an old-fashioned way of lighting up the beach. I was absolutely intrigued to what they were doing, they huddled together and then I could see another flame, they had lit a great fire on the sand, and were now walking down to the shoreline, perhaps they were night fishing. After a while my legs started to ache from standing in one position watching them, and I decided to go an investigate. I put my coat on over my pyjamas and wrapped a scarf around my neck. As I stepped out of the door the wind nearly bowled me over, I put my head down and followed the path to the sea, I stayed back from view to watch the events unfolding before me. In the distance a rowing boat appeared around the end of the rocks, in a matter of minutes it arrived at the shore, the group of men waded into the water, and then I could see what was happening, they were unloading boxes and packages from the small boat. Each man carried one or two boxes and as they turned, I realised they were heading my way. I am not sure who or where, but a voice warned me to be cautious, and not be my normal nosey self. Whatever was going on I did not want to be part of it, I could hear them behind me, laughing and shouting, their accents were so heavy, I couldn't make out one word they were saying. I reached the croft just as they left the beach. Something about them made me feel slightly alarmed,

I could hear them marching up the pathway, they were getting rowdy, they were not people I would want to meet, here on my own on a winter's night. I hoped they would walk straight past the croft, I held my breath as they reached the gate, but no they stopped outside, I couldn't make out what they were saying, but a moment later they were hammering on the front door, the whole croft vibrated and I thought the door would surely collapse under the pressure of their fists. And then as quickly as they arrived, they seemed to dissolve into the night. I cannot imagine what is happening here and what I am getting caught up in. I slightly open the door and cautiously peer through the small gap, the snowfall has covered the path and there is only one set of footprints, and they are mine, leading straight inside. Puzzled I close the door and as I turn back into the room, I can see wet footprints across the stone floor, they stop in the centre of the room, these are not mine, my boots are on the doormat and I am barefoot.

This is my first night here on the island and already I am not sure whether I am losing my senses, what has just happened? without witnesses how do I know, what's real or just my vivid imagination, which constantly teeters on the edge of reality. Tomorrow is a new day and I am sure I will feel different once I have rested, things have been really strained recently, I remind myself, that is why I came here.

THE AWAKENING.

The view from the croft never ceases to lift my fragile heart, at times it makes me quite breathless. I cannot believe that I was ever able to function without this stark beauty right here beneath my feet.

This place is so distant and completely opposite from my previous go at life, I am being constantly bombarded with untold natural simplicity, such a humble prescription to soothe a sad soul that is starting to search for a new pathway.

Let me describe to you what I am feasting my eyes upon, yes, eyes that had grown accustom to the blinding rat race of the great concrete metropolis, and eyes that are constantly filled with warm tears, and a brain without a delete button.

Here on this island, at the furthest tip of this country the evening sun resembles a golden sphere, greater than I have ever seen, there is nothing to mar the view, no tall buildings or pollution, just the vast expanse of the unruly North Sea and a cosmic canopy of the universe towering above me. The golden bruised evening sky has washed the white painted walls of the croft with a soft hue of bluey pink, the constantly changing sea has a wonderful rippling golden movement as the tide changes and starts to ebb, dragging, sucking the water out and away from the sandy beach. The piercing golden rays bursting from the setting sun has changed the moorland behind me, the autumn bracken glows with this dying light and the craggy rock pools on the beach omit a glow likened to bowls of golden nectar.

As the evening gradually changes into night, something within the fabric of the old stone walls appears to omit a long grumbling groan, and then the whole croft sighs, a sound that is quite new to me, and I hope I will eventually become used to it.

Standing at this window that overlooks the beach and the ocean beyond, I am bathed in an eerie aura, nothing to do with the hand of man, just the universe's beautiful natural sunset, completely free, there for the looking, another new discovery for me.

Now, I have time to stop and look at what is right in front of my eyes without any distractions, I am finding surprising comfort in the simplest of things, I also think I am coping better with the unwelcome thoughts that still burst into my mind without warning, thoughts that are like a video that wants to keep playing, reminding me of the reasons that encouraged me to come here.

The vibrant dying light forces itself into the room and settles into the dusty corners, turning cobwebs into gossamer thread, dancing in the mirrors and illuminating the photographs on the wall, giving life to the smiling faces of loved ones, that are captured in time.

The sea is now flaming under the orange sun which is burning the landscape with a surreal afterglow, and then just as magically, a noisy silence that makes your eardrums pop, before straining to hear something to remind you, that you are not the only person living on this island. There is a stillness to my world as the lifegiving sun descends from view, traveling on its eternal orbital path to bring a bright awakening dawn to sleeping countries on the other side of this amazing globe.

The logs on the burner spark and crackle a reminder for me to fetch more wood from the log store, situated at the side of the house. Luckily, I don't have to go out into the wild and forage for wood, part of the lease agreement for this place, was that for the winter, the landlord would provide me with logs and kindling. I think he was pleased to rent this out for the winter when it would normally stay vacant until the spring.

I arrived here a month ago and yet I feel I know the place really well, it sits comfortably in my soul and yet it is hundreds of miles away from my previous life, before all that sadness and lost love, this place is just verging on the edge of wild living, but something deep down inside me feels it is so right, it is positive and hopeful, and for the first time in two years, I can feel a little light to my life and perhaps for the first time in the whole of my life I am finding a deep satisfaction in nature. This is enough for me. This move to the wilderness isles was an immense step, taken after failing to live a normal life and going against every piece of advice given by caring friends,

I decided to follow my instinct and fulfil my ambition to live in this sacred beautiful place. They could not feel my grief or my hunger to leave, some people can stay in the same place that great sadness has happened, not me, I cannot live being constantly reminded of such sorrow on a daily basis, witnessing the home of years of laughter and love turn into an empty meaningless strange place without my soul mate, friends cannot feel my pain they say I am running away or in denial and it will get better with time, I haven't got that time, I need to be a single widow and get used to my new self, away from all that makes me miss my family. Here no one knows me or my life, as they say I share no baggage. The only cargo I have here is stacked in bags and boxes in every room, making the whole place appear so much smaller than it is. I feel I am an empty soul, ready to be filled with new experiences that can give me a reason to trust and enjoy life again.

In just a few weeks, this place, that on first sight felt, deserted and barren, has become bursting with life, not so much human existence, but welcoming natural life, and as a complete surprise I recently found a slight touch of unnatural afterlife, apart from the eerie sounds the house makes at sunset, and the band of noisy drunken men that trudge past the croft, there is something far more unsettling, on occasions I can hear a voice whispering, so softly that I cannot really understand what they are saying, or even if they are really human, at first I thought it was the sea gently sifting the shingle, down on the beach, the other odd occurrence that has started to baffle me, is a young girl appears as if by magic on the rocks overlooking the sea, it can be early in the morning or late at night, so you can only just make out her outline, one minute she's there and then like a fox, she blends into the countryside and vanishes. I am not usually one who delves into the supernatural, but there is something happening here that I cannot explain. I am not frightened of many things these days, once you have seen things that freeze your heart it is hard to find emotion about anything, so I regard the strange voices and the sight of the elusive girl on the rocks as either my mental illness or something that happens when you are susceptible to anything the world wants to present you with, is this madness, who knows.

The croft is centuries old and when the island was a bustling sheep farming and herring fishing community it was a store house for the fisherman, compact and basic but built with tremendously thick stone walls to keep out the long Shetland winters. Even now the croft is still owned by a so-called Lord of the manor who apparently lives on the island in a salubrious farmstead, he rents out the crofts on his estate to the likes of me, a city dweller who wants to taste wild living.

Back in London the estate agent looked me up and down over his condescending spectacles, he warned me about the lack of just about everything in the rental, and that it was really only a summer let, at that time I was standing looking down on him wearing my red soled three-inch heels and sporting a smart suit that cost at least a month of his salary, he only saw the shiny shuck of me, he hadn't met the broken nut inside, the real me willing to give up those shoes and that lifestyle that meant nothing, in reality, it was all materialistic clutter that portrayed nothing except the ability to join the consumer race and fill the pockets of the greedy pedlars.

He said, as I had requested the croft for a long let of twelve months, he would have to consult the owner, I emphasised the fact that I would be willing to pay the full rental for that time and I would be no trouble. He agreed to phone me as soon as possible, but sometimes the owner was hard to locate as he was an artist and writer and was not always ready to be disturbed, hence all the rules about no contact for future tenants, everything must go through the agent. He sounded like a bit of a hermit. That would be fine by me, the less I saw of people the better.

Weeks went by and just when I thought I would never escape London and all it stood for, the agent contacted me and said he had drawn up a contract which was waiting for me to sign and I could take on the rental from the first day of November. Everything then happened so quickly. I rented out my house and cleared my life of clutter, much to the annoyance of my friends, I refused to give them a forwarding address and said when I was feeling more sociable, I would contact them but for the moment I needed my space, not really many of them understood and I am afraid I caused offence to many, but I was really unable to cope with their unhelpful attitudes to my grief, I never once asked for advice, sometimes all I needed was for someone to listen. Then, as I was going completely off my trolley with no-one to stop me, I bought a VW camper van, not a vintage one, it was so well equipped with everything I could possibly need for my new adventure and for my new way of life.

It took me what seemed a lifetime to drive here in the camper, I have been used to having a zippy eco car for my short journeys around London and the furthest that I have ever driven was the Home Counties, that was when I wasn't a widow.

I eventually arrived at the ferry port and stupidly had just missed the only sailing for that evening, I was so exhausted I didn't care, and was grateful for the van being equipped with a bed and blue loo. I spent the next day familiarising myself with the locals and visiting their quaint shops, filling my bags with expensive essentials just in case the croft was more remote than I realised.

The next evening, I was first in the queue and drove straight onto the small ferry, I did not look back, even though I was quite stressed and a bit nervous I was determined to see this adventure through, after all what was the worst thing that could happen and hadn't that happened already. The crossing was smooth but, went on forever and I found it impossible to sit still, the only sounds I could hear was a dull grumbling coming from the heavy engines down below in the bowels of the ship, that were working hard to push the boat through the dark waters, up on the deck a swirling wet mist shrouded the few passengers that could not sleep, I put my hood up over my damp hair and strained my heavy eyes hoping to see some lights from the distant shore or at least a lone star in the cloudy sky.

After what seemed a monotonous few hours, a slight colour change heralded the lazy sunrise, slowly at first and then a glow that burst through the dark clouds and there at last before us in the distance was the bright lights of the welcoming ferry dock.

Abruptly the ship changed direction and maneuvered the iron hulk into docking position, we were all summoned to return to our vehicles. I looked around at the other passengers they all appeared as weary as I felt. I was quite impatient queuing to wait my turn to drive on-shore and it seemed ages before I was signalled to drive off the ramps. Once on land I still had a short journey across the island to the next ferry port which would take me to my final destination. I pulled into the nearest layby and consulted my sat-nav but there was no signal, finding my map book I got a rough idea which direction I should be heading in, luckily the next ferry port was well sign-posted. I arrived in good time for the crossing, this ferry was much smaller than the one I had just travelled on and was already taking on cargo destined for the next island. I stayed with the van and tried to wait patiently for the end of my journey. The morning sky appeared just as grey and misty as it had been for the last few days, a slight fine drizzle had settled on the windscreen and the calm sea was the same colour as the sky. My mood lifted as ahead of me I could see the whole landscape open up in front of me, changing so much from the dreary foggy mainland, I was amazed at the soft rise and falls of the rolling green hills and the burnt hues of the autumn moorland. The Ferry crossing took no time at all and before I knew it, I was back in the van waiting to drive off to my final destination. I was quite surprised at how many people were arriving on foot and wondered if they lived on the island or are like me arriving for a winter break.

A row of taxi's was waiting and quite a few passengers took them. I followed one, which seemed to be going in the same direction as I was. The scenery was amazing, nothing like I've ever seen before. It was a job to keep my eyes on the road, the hills appeared smooth and hundreds of grazing sheep made the barren landscape come alive. The taxi in front of me accelerated and I lost sight of it. Eventually the sign post I had been looking for appeared and I drove the camper off of the concrete roads, and down a rugged lane signposted to Blakes bay, I was relieved that at last I was to reach my final destination. I was tired, but also excited to have come near to finishing my journey, that seemed to have begun such a long time ago. I carefully followed the written instructions the agent had given me, with a warning that it was quite remote and my nearest neighbour was two miles away and there was a weak intermittent mobile phone signal, I think the poor man was frightened for me. He found it hard to understand that this was exactly what I had wanted. After going up steep hills and down uneven dips, I realised I had driven to the edge of beyond, and after the thirty-minute uncomfortable journey across the island, I knew the agent was right and I was going to be isolated from everything, except the wildlife I had read so much about. I suddenly became excited as I drove through a small hamlet made up of a church and a few shops, and then again, when I saw the brake lights of the taxi that was in front of me, turn into a lay by and there on the grass verge was a quaint farm shop. The taxi drove up behind the shop and I saw a large farmhouse in the far distance, I wondered if they were my nearest neighbours. Then I left all forms of civilisation, the landscape became barren as the long uneven road suddenly trundled downwards towards a cove. Ahead of me a mass of mirrored silver stretched out as far as the eye could see, I was so busy looking at the view that I nearly missed the small white croft nestled under the hillocks and rocks. And just for that moment I felt so close to the place and I knew that it was where I could try and repair my fragile mind.

LEAVE YOUR THOUGHTS WITH YESTERDAY.

Night-time is casting its shadow over the sea and moorland, chattering sea birds have arrived onto the shoreline to feed before the light disappears completely, they sing a haunting song in the failing light. I have bought so many reference books with me, mainly on walking and wildlife and of course foraging, which I am looking forward to as long as I don't poison myself with fungi, I only say this because all the books I have read so far, give me a gruesome warning about someone who picked a basket full of free fungi and then died a violent and painful death within minutes, and there was no antidote in the whole wide world. I will stick to what I can recognise from the book or the internet, which I can get a signal for on a good day, if I stand up on the crop of rocks in the bay.

 Some of the windows in the cottage have blinds some do their job and others have long ceased to be of any use and have been tied up with fisherman's twine, not attractive but this is the back of beyond.

I have brought indoors a basket full to the brim of well-seasoned logs collected from the outside store, unfortunately disturbing a variety of scurrying wildlife, it was so dark in the lean-to anything could be lurking out there, I quite ruffled myself, when something at the back of the store moved and my imagination then tricked me into believing I could hear someone breathing heavily, strangely these days I have no idea what is real or what is not. I stoked, the log burner and shut it down, for the night, it should keep in for quite a few hours, the orange flames dance and cast a flickering light across the stone floor.

Unfolding the ancient sofa bed, I roll out my duvet and rescue my pillow from the floor, the flagstones beneath my feet are as cold as the artic, I hop into bed quickly and soon find myself warm and cosy, considering today I have been idle, and have done literally nothing, yet I am extremely tired. The warmth of the fire and the togs of the duvet take me off into a land of imagination and dreams. Just before I succumbed to the grips of unconsciousness, far, far away perhaps in my dreams a voice calls me, 'Alice, Alice, where are you?' they repeat the question, I rouse myself and sleepily reply, 'I am here. I fall into a night of jumbled dreams that make no sense at all, occasionally I stir and wake myself up and then I remember why I am here and I try not to remind myself of, 'the then,' and all the heartbreak that goes with it. In my sleepy head I say, 'That was then and this is now. Please let me just forget, for a while.' I have been trying to stop the never-ending movie that wants to invade my recovery and keep constantly playing in my mind. I am so weary of waking at some ungodly hour, to find my face streaked with night terror tears and then when I am beyond the possibility of returning to sleep, I am bombarded with all the inappropriate questions that my mind wants to ask me, the latest being, 'What were my last words to Luca on that fateful day.' I can see him as clearly as if he was here, he was walking out through the front door, jangling his car keys and laughing, he said he would take his car as mother didn't like squeezing herself into my little smart car. I punish myself by racking my brain, did I say goodbye, take care, I love you, or was I too busy with all the preparations for the Christmas dinner, I am sad I will never know what he thought, what he said, if anything when he was trapped in the wreckage. They sent someone to fetch me but by the time I arrived, it was too late for both of them, they had left their mangled shells behind them, only I remained breathing, waiting, watching, staring at a white sheet covering Luca's car. Knowing that under that cover were the only two people that my life stood for. Hell proceeded.

It's quite dark when I wake and today, I am going to go out for an early morning trek and get some perspective on my surroundings. The kettle takes forever to whistle and I decide not to shower, until I have had at least two cups of coffee. Somewhere hidden in one of the boxes stacked against the wall I have a modern electric kettle and a coffee machine; I am assured the generator outside can cope with a few electrical items as long as I don't put them on all at the same time. I will have to get to grips with unpacking, as the utensils in the kitchen are ancient and quite useless.

The windows quickly steam up with the warmth from the slow old-fashioned kettle and suddenly the quiet is shattered by the shrill intrusion of the whistle that informs me that the water is ready for that long yearned for coffee. I can wait for breakfast, today I am eager to explore the island a little bit further. I have tried to dress in reasonably appropriate clothing, I have ordered a wet weather anorak and walking boots from the one and only general store back in the small village, the shop keeper informed me that it could take a while as they would have to come from the mainland. I said I was planning to be here for a while and I would wait, normally I would just sit at my laptop and order whatever I wanted and before you knew it a man would knock at the door with the order, I had completely forgotten about shops.

I closed and locked the rickety weather-beaten door behind me and slipped the giant key into my pocket, checking that the small guide book of island walks was in my other pocket. The tide was coming in and a sea breeze lifts my hair, a wet mist threatened to excite my wavy hair into a frenzy of fuzzy curls that no brush could ever tame. I startled a group of shore birds; I am still learning about the wildlife but I do think these might have been Lapwings. The book I found on a shelf in the croft, is a little observer book of, 'The Seashore,' dated 1954, the trekking book is a little later, I found it in the village store where they had a stand of second-hand books, I also bought a book on discovering Shetland history, which I have yet to read.

The sun is not going to show its face today and is hidden behind rolling grey clouds, there is so much sky here, as far as you can see stretching from east to west with nothing in the way to stop it. In London the sky is hidden by tall buildings which cast long shadows, there are parks but, in the summer, they become extremely busy, all the harsh concrete of the city acts as a giant storage heater so at lunch time workers stream out of their offices and snatch an hour in the shade of the trees vying for a patch of grass.

The sea and the sky blend into each other, gentle waves are silently lapping the sand, the birds keep moving back onto dry land, a seagull soars high and drops a mussel onto the rocks, it splits open and the gull dives and deftly takes the exposed crustacean.

I continue to walk up the craggy path worn by endless hikers and sheep, which seem to be everywhere you look, cotton wool bundles with matchstick legs, painted onto the distant hillside canvas. The closest ones lazily turn their heads to look at me, but soon bury their noses back into the grass of the moorland, so strange for a large animal to eat such small amounts at a time, no wonder they graze all day. In the windswept hedgerows that lean towards the headland I catch site of a grey furry creature, could be a rabbit or a rogue grey squirrel, I think the red squirrel is favoured here, such a shame we cannot let everything live together.

In my other life when I was a wife and a daughter, we lived just outside the city in a tall Victorian town house, the garden was narrow and long, over the years I planted trees and shrubs eventually making it quite a sanctuary for the urban wildlife. I could walk to the end of the garden and not be able to see the house. Secluded amongst the trees we built a summerhouse with a wood-burner so we could use it throughout the year and spent many happy hours reading and watching visiting creatures that were totally unaware of our presence.

I cannot stop my mind from visiting that life, at times I still find it unbelievable that all that has gone and of course memories are all that we are left with. A widow and an orphan in such a short time. I feel as though I am living on another planet or perhaps in a different dimension where nothing will ever be the same, even close friends feel strangely distant and how out of touch they have become, death of a partner puts you in a different category seen by some as predatory, where their husbands are concerned, and needy, busy people, who are frightened you might ask them for help, none of these are true in my case, grief has made me independent and wise to what I want from life, also I have become selfish and put my wellbeing first. However harsh this seems I have to look out for number one, to be able to make this trip through life solo. I could write a gloomy book about the advice and reactions of friends and relations when you lose someone, and of course the guilt that you are made to feel, as if somehow it is your fault, you must have done something to get yourself in this mess.

The drizzling misty rain has gained power and is starting to change into driving heavy drops accompanied by a cool blustery wind, my vision is obscured by my wet hair that has escaped from my loose hood and stuck to my face. Above me is a group of grass covered hillocks and I can just about make out a few bedraggled sheep sheltering. I push myself forward and eventually feel the wind subside as I shelter in the space between the rocks. I cannot wait for my real waterproof clothing to arrive; a trickle of icy water has found its way into the back of my coat and is following a straight path down my spine settling into the top of my jeans. Great bruised clouds roll speedily over the hill so close that everything below has vanished into the white mist. I move around in the lee of the wind and see something that I hadn't noticed before, just a few yards from me stands the ruins of a small chapel, there is no roof or windows but the stone walls are intact. I step through the doorway and find the dense stonework really protects me from the wind. This is the furthest I have walked since I arrived and am pleased to discover something new. The clouds pass swiftly and suddenly the weak sunshine pierces the gloom and turns the sea into an ocean of mercury. I cannot possibly get any wetter; I walk slowly down the hill retracing my earlier footsteps. I feel lighter and know that walking in the wild is not only exhilarating but healing mentally and physically. I am starting to believe I have done the right thing to come to this magical place where I can put myself back into order.

 By the time I reach in my pocket for the large key I am so uncomfortable, my jeans have shrunk over my thighs and I feel about to burst out of them, as I turn to close the door something catches my eye. The girls there again, standing up on the headland looking out to sea, where in heavens name did, she come from, there was no-one out there when I was walking and there isn't another cottage for miles. I forget about changing my wet clothes and go back outside and think perhaps she's in some sort of trouble. The last thing I need is to get caught up in anyone else's problem but something must be wrong, who in their right mind other than me would venture out on a day like today without a coat. I walk up the slope and as I get nearer, I see, she is a lot younger than me. She is wearing a pale blue midi dress with sprigs of white daisies on, not really appropriate for this climate and yet she doesn't appear to be cold. As I reach the grassy top, she turns to face me, her eyes are forget-me-not blue, but as cold as ice, she stares into my face but does not see me, she is far away watching something I cannot see. My blood runs cold and chills my heart, her mouth opens and closes, saying words I cannot hear, she is whispering the same thing over and over again, I cannot understand what she is saying. My mouth is so dry and I find it hard not to flee, my sensible mind takes over and is cross for my stupidity, she's just a girl, no threat. 'Can I help you; you must be cold.' I wait for an answer, she walks towards me and I step aside as she silently passes. She must be real, the breeze blows her golden locks, her fine dress floats as she glides down the hill, in the direction of the croft. I trot after her surprised about the way she's heading. She hesitates for a moment at the croft door which is wide open, and then she's inside. I reach the front door in seconds and am ready to find out, what is wrong with this person. I cannot believe she is nowhere to be found, nervously I search every crook and cranny, every moment expecting to find her, I even stupidly look in the cupboards, nothing. Confused as to what has just happened, I close the front door and securely lock it. Somewhere, in the croft, something inhuman takes a deep grumbling breath, the whole croft vibrates and shudders like an earth tremor, I wait, nothing happens. I wonder what in heavens name has just taken place, no-one would ever believe me if I told them, so I think I must keep all of this to myself at the moment.

The light is starting to fail and I light my oil lamps, black smelly smoke spirals into the cold room. I place the lamps on the window sills, reflecting a warm glow into the world outside and giving me some light to the dark corners. What a strange thing to happen. I am glad the log basket is full and I don't have to go outside tonight.

I feel unsettled, I don't need or want any-more strange events in my life, was the girl real, if so where did she go and why did she act so oddly. I know all about mental illness I have first-hand knowledge of crazy. Life can run smoothly for some people all their lives and they have no idea of the fine line between sanity and madness and how the strongest of folk can suddenly become so broken, their life shattered into so many pieces that to restore is totally impossible, sometime it's the brains way of telling us that it needs a rest and cannot cope.

I am going to try and take my mind off today's strange events, and make myself unpack some of the boxes that are stacked around the place, besides I really need some of the provisions I bought with me, so far, I have been surviving on bits and pieces I bought from the shop at the entrance to the large farm a few miles back towards the town. They seem to have most things you need, fresh veg, local caught seafood, meat, fish and a freezer full of homemade pies and casseroles, expensive but quite delicious.

I slice through the sticky tape that I over zealously double sealed the boxes with, a slight feeling of excitement tickles my insides as I pull open the lid to reveal my belongings and then, a moment of sadness as I pull out precious photographs, a silent warm tear trickles down my cold cheek, I am always so surprised how quickly they come and how easily they flow. I put the picture of Luca and me happy, laughing, enjoying a family occasion, onto the dresser where I can see him and talk to him. I swear his eyes follow me wherever I am in the room as he would have done when he was alive. Next out of the box a well-stocked first aid kit, needles and thread, notepad and envelopes and a selection of blank postcards which I fully intend to paint scenes from the islands on and send to no-one in particular. My knees are going to sleep and my toes are tingling, I get up and pull open another box hoping to find the coffee machine and its pods. Luck at last my lovely black and chrome lifesaver is sitting proudly on the kitchen worktop, and six-months supply of pods are stored on the empty shelf above it. Too tempting to ignore I set the switches in motion and then this magical machine grumbles coughs and splutters, and just as the monster in it spits froth the air is filled with the magical insomniac steam, and for a moment I am at peace with the view of the almost black sea and my equally dark coffee.

The shelf in the kitchen now looks like a shop, four cartons of long-life milk and an extremely large bag of raw porridge oats, something I've never made but it seemed to be the right kind of thing to bring to the Shetlands, I am more used to sachets that you mix with hot water, but now I should have time to go back to the good old days, next to the porridge is Self-Raising flour, a packet of dried yeast and my mother's battered bread tin, she always said it was a therapy to make real bread from scratch, and if she was ever cross with my dad the bread was always bigger and better than when she was in a good mood. I have bought a variety of dried pulses with me and wind tablets which I am sure I will need after the vast amount of lentils on the shelf.

I read in a survival book that some ready meals you buy from a camping shop are a good standby for when the weather closes in, so I have bought enough to see me through the days when the snow stops me from leaving, I have hotpot, shepherd's pie, chilli con carne, I can honestly say not one of them appeals to my delicate pallet, but if I am stranded here in a six-foot snow drift then I would not starve.

Recently I have noticed my feelings of grief are not quite as extreme as they have been, at one time the feeling of disbelief to what had happened would overwhelm and paralyse me into the upmost feeling of isolation and despair, with a longing for my old life back again, friends didn't know how to help so they stayed away, I don't blame them I was not good company and all for a really good reason, the two people who would comfort me in times of crisis had gone. I could be lonely and lost in a room full of people, every well-meaning soul had a different piece of advice on how to get over my loss. I realise you don't get over your grief, so I stopped trying, in those early dark days you bumble along getting through one day at a time, and gradually you live alongside your loss, because it will always be there and will never go away. People who have never lost their soul mate cannot grip your sadness, and are impatient for you to get over it, so you avoid them and they do the same with you, and friends who are divorced and glad to be rid of their men cannot understand your attitude to loss and ask, 'Hope he left you well off,' or 'Don't worry you'll find someone else,' and, 'At least you know where he is, and he hasn't run off with another women,' this is why I am here, to find out who I am, now, I have never been, just Alice, I am not a daughter or a wife anymore.

The night sky has drawn itself over the land and all the colours of the island are muted into sleep. A shrill scream rents through the night, far away up in the hills a fox calls a mate, it is now a time for the night creatures to live their time unseen by man.

I finish unpacking the box and am pleased to find my battery radio and torch, at the bottom of the carton is a canvas bag containing a small box of paints, watercolour paper and a variety of painting brushes. I have the intention to travel to the top of the cliffs on the other side of the island and paint the world as I see it. I am not a good painter more after the style of a blind Lowry/5-year-old. Tomorrow I hope the elusive girl stays away and I can get on with whatever my unstable mind decides to do, for now I am going to toast the last of the crumpets and slather them with Scottish butter and empty the contents of a miniature jar of honey on them, and in the morning, I will wash the jar out to use for painting, for when I become a travelling island artist.

I am pleased to snuggle into the duvet as the croft cools down so quickly once the fire dies, my ears strain to a sound in the distance that is getting louder and louder and coming upwards from the beach, I sit up straining my ears to listen. Footsteps are crunching on the shingle, getting closer and closer to the croft. I hold my breath as they stop at the door. It seemed an age before they crunched their way around the outside walls, I listen as the steps stop outside the windows. I could hardly bare the crunching sound, as they stomped heavily around the side of the building and then they ceased completely. It was ages before I stopped straining my ears to listen for the footsteps, I pulled the covers up over me and tried to sleep, I was so cold and so wide awake.

NATURE BLOWS YOUR MIND.

Today I am collecting my walking clothes from the shop, this means taking the van out which has been idle for a few weeks. She starts first time, the windscreen is completely clouded by the salt that blows in off the sea, it takes a good few pints of screen wash to remove the salty soup. The journey is really quite pleasant, the land dips and rises as I travel on the ancient road, well worn by man over centuries of time, all history now, as, we will be someday, when our journey is done. The road is not smooth nor straight but pot-holed and bumpy, I drive through rocky overhangs and then open moorland and my soul is lifted by the complete nothingness each side of me, perhaps if I looked really hard, I could see sheep and the occasional sea gulls soaring high above the cliffs in the azure blue sky. The weather is cold but crisp and clear, a good day to breathe in the coming winter that sits just around the corner.

The small village feels overwhelming after spending time in the sanctuary of the croft. I have a list with me of all the things I need to purchase. The cheerful lady behind the counter is exceptionally friendly, I find it difficult to understand her strong island accent and keep saying sorry, she is considerate and slows her speech and pronounces her words as if I am deaf. I realise she hasn't stopped smiling and I like her instantly. She asks a few questions but obviously knows a little bit about me, she asks am I a widow, and before I can answer she says she has been a widow for a while and adds, 'Be kind to yourself, it will change slowly, there are no rules with grief, time will give you distance.' I cannot answer for fear of melting into tears when people are too nice to me.

My coat has arrived and she shows me all the different layers that un-popper when the weather changes, or if I find it too warm. I am amazed how lightweight it is and the hood is lined with fleece and a drawstring keeps it snug. The boots are amazing and again have thermal liners. I part with an extortionate amount of money and pick up my new island wear, just as I was about to leave, I remembered the strange girl on the rocks. I asked did she know who she could possibly be, instantly she replied that there was no-one living within 2 miles of the croft, the nearest being the owner of my home, Simon Blake, who resided at the Weathercote farm up on the hill, and he lived on his own, apart from the housekeeper and her husband who was the farm manager for the estate, Tom Grover and his wife Betty also manned the farm shop selling local produce. I told her I had met them, and I asked what my landlord was like, she said, he was a bit of a recluse and not many people saw him in the village, he was an author and illustrator and did not encourage anyone to visit, sometimes he was away a for long lengths of time and the house would be closed up, the Grover lived in a cottage on the estate and looked after the place. I thanked her for my clothes and bundled my shopping onto the back seat of the van, my next stop was the hardware shop.

A large brass bell clanged noisily when I entered the aladdins cave, the shop was like something from the past, from floor to ceiling and across the beams hung copper pots, kettles and kitchenware that belonged in the last century if not before. On the tightly stacked shelves were boxes of nails, screws of every size imaginable and you could purchase a single one instead of a plastic bag of a hundred as we usually do, all I wanted was some batteries for my radio and a small flask so I could take hot coffee out on my walks. After answering what seemed like a questionnaire, I managed to persuade the shop keeper to let me have the items and leave.

I drove on to the end of the small row of shops and was surprised to see a light on in the small hall beside the church, there were quite a few cars parked outside, which made it quite difficult for me to turn the van around. A kindly lady saw my plight and offered to guide me backwards, I wound down my window to thank her, she informed me that it wasn't usually this busy but the local history society were having their monthly meeting and added as I looked new to the area perhaps, I would like to join them, as their numbers were dwindling owing to the demise of some of the older members. I said it sounded great but at the moment I was a little busy, she jotted down her name and phone number and said to ring her if I wanted to go to next month's meeting, she would give me all the details, I thanked her and escaped, I still find it hard to listen to people talking trivia, and I get so impatient with many normal things. I am pleased to get away from reality and take the quiet picturesque journey back to my haven.

The green hills roll away from the road, a faint purple hue washes across the heathland as the heather fades into autumn. Suddenly out of the corner of my eye I catch a flash of amber, I stupidly try to steer the van and at the same time cast my eyes to look at the movement in the heather, but forget to look in my rear view mirror and then I see a car approaching at great speed, a loud blaring horn brings me back to my senses as a black shiny Range rover overtakes me, barely squeezing past and then when I brake hard and pull the wheels over to the right side of the road the arrogant man puts his brakes on, and nearly says goodbye to the back of his car. I stop the van and watch the driver's door open; I quickly lock my door and wind the window up. I physically hunch my shoulders and wait for the onslaught, even though I know I was in the wrong, he was driving like an idiot, he should have more consideration for any wildlife that could have wandered across the road, and then the new me became enraged and I unlocked the door and was out of the van striding towards this maniac and I met him half way. Before this scruffy long-haired idiot could open his mouth, I gave him a good lashing with my tongue on driving in the countryside, and the look on his whiskered face told me it had had the desired effect. If he thought he was going to bully me then he was quite mistaken. When the red mist subsided, I could see that the silent man was pushing something towards me, I quickly stepped back, it could be a gun or knife, after all I came from London, no he stood with my purse in his hand. I snatched it and mumbled a thank-you. He spoke, 'You left this in the shop, I tried to catch you up. And thanks for the advice on my driving, I will heed your warning and I think you were unnecessarily unkind; I do have a mother.' Without another word he casually walked back to his car and drove off at a sensible speed. I sat for a while so embarrassed by my behaviour, my friends were right I have changed so much I am not the person I used to know, anger is always just below the surface waiting to escape and scream and scream.

The car was nowhere in front of me, he must have turned off somewhere along the road. I was pleased to reach the croft and seclusion. I had certainly made a fool of myself today, hopefully I'll never meet him on the road again.

I hang my new coat on the hook by the front door and position my shoes underneath, ready for my next walk. I think I'll take my mind off my bad behaviour, and unpack another box, but before I attempt that job, I put new batteries in the radio and tune into a familiar channel, putting a pod in the coffee machine I stand and wait for the delicious steam to swirl around my face, and then sitting on the floor, I open another insight into my past life.

The box contains nothing of excitement, just more tins, sardines, sadly I have never liked them, pilchards, shame I haven't got a cat, and good old corned beef liable to slice and dice your fingers when you try to open it, and then four cans of fly killer as I had been warned about the midges. I really want to find my book on beekeeping, this is something I have always planned to do, I love bees and I love honey, the orchard here looks to be the perfect place to try this out, of course I know that it's not that easy, Luca and I went on a short course to learn how to look after them, it was another of the things we were going to do when we were rich enough to leave the concrete jungle and live in the country, I can still carry out my part of the dream and who knows he might join me. I think also that I could have a small vegetable patch here and some flowers of course. Somewhere hiding in one of the boxes I have Mrs., Beaton's book which should show me how to make preserves and chutneys and a few handy household hints that are most probably quite out of date, but will make interesting reading.

I fight with the ignition on the calor gas cooker and give up, and search for a box of matches that yesterday were on the hearth by the fire. I light a piece of paper from the fire and hurry to the kitchen, the flame blows out each time. One more go before I lose my appetite, I walk really slowly not to cause a draft and throw the burning paper onto the cooker, luckily the gas ignites and a cosy blue flame awaits my can of game soup, to be served with a par cooked ciabatta that is enveloped in a strong casing of the dreaded plastic, which requires a sharp pair of scissors that holiday lets don't have, like no adult cutlery, they only have bendy knives that would do no harm even to a watermelon.

My soup steams in the coolness of the croft, the bread is in the oven and the combined smell of the two is very pleasing to my hungry stomach. The radio is tuned into a channel that we both listened to when we got home from work, it's all wrong and I have to turn it off, I will never ever forget him but some things are not a good reminder, I feel all my energy leave my body, and let my soup go cold, grief has filled my empty stomach. You never know what is going to make your heart bleed, I know it will pass, I give in to warm tears and go with the flow of today, this moment, now. As I reach for the giant box of tissues that have become my constant companion, there is a slight tapping sound, at first, I am not sure where it is coming from, I listen carefully, it seems to be somewhere high above me in the attic, if there is one. Perhaps a squirrel or mouse has made a nest up there, I walk from room to room looking for a loft hatch nothing, going outside I slowly walk right around the place, no sign of anything apart from a skylight window high up near the chimney. I quickly glance into the dark lean-to, apart from a great stack of logs against the wall, I can't see much at all, and then, far back in the shadows and sticky cobwebs I can see a ladder of some sort, it looks like it might lead up to a trap door in the overhang of the roof. There is no way I am crawling through the junk to get to the ladder, hopefully the creature will keep quiet or leave.

I begin another hunt to find the matches as I now fancy some toast, I start another relay with a flaming piece of paper to the cooker and back to the fire, third time lucky, the grill splutters and ignites with a whoosh, luckily, I escape with my eyebrows. It seems that I am waiting ages for the eye level grill to brown the toast, then as it starts to cook the tapping above my head in the loft starts again and then turns into a scratching sound that puts my teeth on edge. I try to ignore the ghastly noise which is quite intermittent, I take my toast into the main room and the noise is more muffled so it must be above the kitchen area.

The inside of the croft is quite compact and has only three rooms, the main bedsitting room, a small kitchenette area, which is down three stone steps, and off of there a bathroom with a shower above the high iron bath, hot water is heated by a temperamental gas boiler that is cleverly squeezed into a tiny space, also a big white china loo, with a cistern high up on the wall with a long chain and handle to pull, and when you pull it Niagara falls gushes down and splashes over the edges, you have to move really quickly else it doubles as a foot bath. All the floors throughout are solid stone which sparkles in the light and is so cold to walk on. The kitchen has a fridge with a small ice compartment, and the laundry facilities are an antiquated automatic washing machine, that could be worth something in a museum, there is no tumble dryer, but a lovely brown wooden clothes horse of Victorian descent. The cupboard under the sink has a metal dustpan and bristleless brush and in a tattered box is a pressure cooker with illegible instructions, I have heard about these contraptions that in the past could explode and blow the windows out of a house, that would be hard to explain to my landlord. I really cannot complain as the croft is not meant for long term living, only as a short-term holiday let for fishermen or fishing-people.

I try again with the radio and tune into an island station broadcast giving out the shipping news, there is a comfort in the gentle accent of the newsreader as he mentions all the familiar areas that we grew up with.

Against a wall behind the sofa is a tall bookcase, I had a brief look the other day, a lot of the books are about fishing and hunting, outdated and horribly cruel, but on closer inspection a few books could be of interest to me, especially the one explaining the history of the island, and another leather bound, handwritten and delicately illustrated, depicting wildlife and fauna, beautiful partly faded watercolour plates adorn the delicate pages with detailed descriptions written in pen and ink, underneath some of the pictures were short poetic verses, now this, did interest me, something I would love to attempt myself. The album is worn and fragile, I carefully turn the pages. The last page has part of a signature on it, I take it over to the light, the back page has lost part of its cover and all I can make out is an artistic italic 'A' and the top of perhaps a P, R or B. I carefully replace it back in the bookcase.

It is late afternoon and shadows are being cast, I am restless, I need to walk, this time of day I always find difficult so I have decided to change it and not sit and dwell on how things used to be, but change the pattern so I am going to try out my new coat and shoes and walk. I have a torch and my phone which is totally useless up here and as I push my arms into my three-layered sarcophagi's I feel like an Egyptian mummy poppered up in my coat, I walk stiffly out of the cottage just in time to see the rear lights of a vehicle go up the track, I check on my van, all's okay, I forget this is the back of beyond and not civilisation where you can lose just about anything in the blink of an eye. I hope it's not a hunter because, in no uncertain terms we would fall out.

I am going to take a different footpath this afternoon, I am going behind the croft where the shingle path winds up the steep hill, I stride out at a steady pace, my thermal coat works well and I have to undo the top poppers, to let some hot air out, I pause for a moment and turn to look down upon the bay, the North Sea has rolled in and covered the rock pools, a few shore birds still remain picking over the stones and sifting through the fine sand and shingle. The shadow of dusk is creeping over the horizon pushing the daylight away. I climb steadily, my calves start to ache as the path becomes quite a lot steeper. The pathway narrows as it trails through a group of untidy rocks, my boots grip the loose stones and I am pleased to finally reach the summit. My heart is racing with exercise and excitement, I am glad to rest a while, I feel I have reached the top of the world, there is no light pollution here and the dusky sky is awesome in its fullness, I sit down on the remains of a dry-stone wall, the view is so breath-taking, to one side the great expanse of the ocean and to the other side the hills away down into the valleys and then beyond just endless nothingness.

I feel comfortable being here totally on my own, free with the thoughts that race through my head and no-one to interrupt me. Something here is giving me a feeling of being so small in something far bigger than I could ever imagine, is this a moment of enlightenment that the Buddhists believe in or is it an acceptance that there is more to life than I will ever understand while I am here on this planet, perhaps it's not for us to know.

The relentless squally wind blows fiercely, only my face is unprotected; I turn away from the blast. Here at the top of the hill I can see a mass of small lights down in the valley resembling a miniature village. Far up on the hillside I can just make out a farm and all of the barns and outbuildings, a steady stream of grey smoke spirals from the tall chimneys of the large house, billowing out into the night air.

The track widens as I cross along the top of the hill, a few clumps of brambles and windswept hedges break up the clearing, once a shelter for the sheep. I am sure in the summer the landscape will change, with wildflowers and grasses that have now died, resting for the long winter. I change direction and start to walk in-land, with every step I tread the scenery changes and I can see far across the island to the mainland in the distance. Beside me in the bracken and brambles I can hear the small night creatures scurrying away from my footsteps, a small rodent crosses my path and dashes for the shelter of a thicket in time to disappear from a barn owl that is hunting low over the hill in front of me. Something deep inside me brings my steps to a halt, I stop to survey the land and feel as though the chain that has enclosed my heart for such a long time has slightly loosened, even though my coat feels heavy I walk onwards feeling my shoulders are a little lighter and inside my head there is a clearness of vision as to what I need in my life, my heart has started to repair the cracks and I feel there is hope for me the first time in a long time. Each step I take is a step forward into a new direction and I know nature is going to play a large part in my recovery, because here with all its unbelievable natural beauty I have started to rest and repair, becoming like the sleeping trees and plants getting ready to grow in the spring.

Perhaps there is a time for mourning and I might be coming to the end of that period, if not perhaps a change in me. You cannot grieve if you have never loved, somehow on this walk I have found clarity, I start to walk back to the croft and face the sunset which is painting the sky in vivid colours, and though I am not religious I believe in the wonders of Ghia and all that live on her, this is a magical sacred moment; I am sure nature is healing me and showing me the truth of the universe. This moment is my turning point, high on this hill not alone but accompanied by all life's creatures, plants, trees, and the everchanging universe, lit by the moon and warmed by the sun, what more do I need.

I tread lightly, I feel oddly different, all is not cold and pointless, a glimmer of hope is all we need to take a step into a journey on your own, I know I will keep moving forward, and I can never go back to that life. That was then and this is now.'

I can hardly see where I am going but I cannot stop and turn around, I am walking and each step is changing my thoughts.

A CATERPILLAR RISES TO BE A BETTER
VERSION OF IT'S SELF.

In the early hours of this morning, I was woken by a noisy, group of hikers walking past, I think they were unaware there was anyone in the croft, they shouted to each other quite loudly, I did get up to look but they were long gone off down to the shore, I think a little later I heard their voices in the distance going in the opposite direction towards the rocks.

I couldn't go back to sleep after the rowdy walkers and as I have many exciting plans racing through my mind, I thought I would make an early start on a new venture.

I have decided I am going to clear some of the garden and get it ready for growing some vegetables, I know it's the wrong time of the year but I read somewhere that you should turn over the ground roughly before the harsh frosts, as the winter ice will help the clods breakdown and aerate the earth ready for spring planting. I had a good rummage through the cobweb infested lean-to and found a few rusty old garden tools at the back, I also discovered the old wooden ladder which leads up to an attic door, that has been well secured with metal bolts and padlocks.

Even though it is December and near to Christmas the weather has been quite kind, but today I can feel the north wind swirling around me like a ghostly chill. I have dressed in a strange combination of clothes and am glad that nobody who knows me will see me. I think I know where the best position in the garden will be for all day sunshine. The garden is surrounded by a stone wall which in places has slipped down, these stones I will use to edge my veg patch. The whole area is covered in a variety of humps of tough grass with roots that reach down into hell. This is going to be a bigger job than I first thought.

My bobble hat has grown in the wild weather and each time I bend over to pull out the grass it insists on slipping down and covering my eyes, and my shocking pink wellies that I bought with me shine like a beacon, not very countryside. I am building quite a heap of grass and mud which I will compost down whatever that means, I will be sure to find out more when I google 'Composting,' I am sure I will soon get the hang of it.

My back wants to cry and my nose is running voluntarily, this north wind is cutting and I decide it must be time for coffee. I look at the pathetic patch of mud that I have cleared, I think this allotment lark is going to be harder that I first thought. I kick off my boots at the door and my heart sinks, that girl is back up on the edge of the rocks she turns and sees me. I wave and think perhaps I'll invite her for coffee, even though she seems a little odd. I keep an eye on her from the window, she doesn't move and just looks out across the sea and beyond. I can't believe how cold she must be without a coat. Slowly she turns around and for a moment her eyes gaze towards the croft, she doesn't come down, but slowly turns her head and then without warning, fades into the countryside, as if the very earth absorbed her.

Oh well, she's missed a smashing cup of fresh coffee. I take my cup back outside and sit it on the wall, I pull on my sticky gloves and return to the patch, the light catches something in the mud I reach for it and am surprised it is a muddy chain with a clod of earth on the end. I take it to the outside pump and try to rinse the mud from it. The chain sparkles and is a gold colour, and then such a pleasant surprise, on the end under the clod of mud is a gold locket, battered and dented by its muddy grave, I try to open it, but the clasp is well and truly jammed, plus my gloves are soaking wet and I cannot feel my fingers. Inside I rinse the treasure under the tap and find a knife from the drawer, the vegetable knife has the thinnest blade. Holding the locket in a tea towel I use the technique recommended for opening oysters, after a couple of attempts the soft gold gives way and the hinged door opens. I take it to the light from the window and am surprised but baffled by the photo, it is sepia and marked by age but is quite obvious to who this lady is, if I am not mistaken, she is the incredible likeness of the girl on the rocks, she must be a relation. In the opposite side of the locket is a picture of a dog, a black and white collie. The girl appears to be dressed in fancy dress, clothes from a long time ago. What an interesting mystery, I put it in a drawer of the dresser for safe keeping, and if ever I get to meet the illusive girl, I will give it to her.

The wind is blowing the foam off of the wild sea and frothy suds are falling like snow, I persevere with the digging until the wind is roaring in my face, blinding me. I give in with gardening and decide to capture the unceasing crashing waves with my camera, with the view of one day painting the wildness. My hood string is tied tightly under my chin and my camera is around my neck. It is extremely difficult to keep standing upright and I battle forward against the angry wind, the sand from the beach blasts into my face and I close my eyes not sure at all if this is a good idea. I tuck myself against a small mound of jagged rocks and manage to open my eyes. I must have taken a few dozen photographs of the sea and spray and I really hope they all come out when I put them onto my computer. I think the storm has set in for the day and the next high tide will surely be a noisy one.

I am back indoors and still the sound of the thrashing sea can be heard even through these thick walls. I know how dangerous the ocean can be, but there is something absolutely compelling about its total disregard for anyone or anything in its way and deserves great respect as it can be kind or a killer. The rain is now beating at the window and marring the view, time for more unpacking. I decide to find out which box is hiding the adaptor for my camera in and also, I need to get rid of these boxes that are cluttering up the place, I will flatten them as I might need them if I ever leave.

The box contains tea cloths and bath towels, which in-between I have carefully tucked breakable objects.

Carefully I pull out the cables I needed and unpack more linen to discover my ear-phones and antiquated Walkman so I can listen to music whilst I walk and I can also dictate on it, old fashioned but just as useful as my phone, at least I only need batteries for my Walkman and not an invisible elusive signal that supposedly travels through thin air, I know what I prefer. The absence of communications from the outside world is quite a blessing, there is a fat bodied television sitting in the corner and a skew-whiff aerial dangling from the roof, but I am hesitant to turn it on because I know that the world news will not be happy and at the moment I am coping with my own bad news and don't want my head filled with every tragedy in the world, I just cannot cope and need to be switched off so I can digest and recover. I am starting to be in a better place so must avoid any setbacks. I have been vulnerable and a sponge for every sad tale everyone wants to tell me.

In the box are also a few dozen favourite cassettes that are my soul music, such a dated way of listening to music but again no signal needed.

My supper tonight is beautiful local caught salmon fillets with a lemon and samphire sauce. The farm shop sells all local caught fish and meat and a variety of seasonal and unseasonable fruit and vegetables. The meat I steer a little clear of only because one day I could be watching the deer and the hares and the next day I could be eating them, I am a coward if I had to kill the creatures myself, I would be a vegetarian but as I expect others to kill it, I readily eat it. One day I will give myself a good talking to.

The wind is still howling and trying to come in through the ill-fitting windows, I know if I complain to the agent, he will remind me that this croft is only supposed to be rented out for the summer and is not really suitable for the winter, it is all written in my lengthy contract and he knows how desperate I was to rent this haven. I can put up with anything just to stay here.

The steam from the poaching salmon smells delicious but mists up the windows, I slightly open the small skylight in the kitchen and smile at how the wind sounds like someone crying, the blind on the window acts like a harp and sings a mournful song, in the end I can't stand the sound any longer and close the window. There is no moonlight tonight and the darkness has come early, I light a candle which is enough light to eat by, the salmon is delicious and I finish it off with a fresh coffee, sadly no dessert, I hope in the summer the trees in the orchard will bear fruit so I can make fresh fruit pies and crumbles.

I am now completely sedated with food and pleasantly comfortable, I search through the bookcase for something to read, I think many paper backs have been left by previous holiday makers and are of no interest to me. A large book at the bottom of the shelf attracts my eye it is dusty and the red leather cover has seen better days. I have to sit at the table as the book is too big to read on my lap. In the dim light I can't make out the title so put on the table lamp and stretch the cable across to the table. The book is musty and the distinct smell that old books emits irritates my nose. There is no title on the cover and the gold leaf pages have long lost their gilding. The pages are thin like tissue paper and printed in an old-fashioned script, the ink has faded in some places but as I read on, I discover the book is a history of the

Blake family, the owners of this place and by the look of the map also a large part of this island. There is a double page inside the front cover folded over and where the crease is it is thin and worn, it appears too fragile to unfold and I would hate to be the one who destroys this fine document. I sift through the book selecting particular pages, it is not as interesting as I hoped it would be, I soon tire of all the small words and think that I will save it for when I am in the mood for a serious read.

Somewhere in one of the bags I have left in the back of the camper are a few seed catalogues I picked up from a nursery on one of my many visits. In the early days when I was still stunned by events and used to get maudlin and overwhelmed with fear, I would get myself out of the house every day and walk, anywhere would do, I would walk every supermarket putting useless items into the trolley, I would walk with my head down not making any eye contact with anyone for fear of someone talking to me, then I realised most people who recognised me went out of their way to avoid me, perhaps they thought death is catching. One friend said she had avoided me as she did not want to remind me of my dead family. I replied kindly, you could never remind me because how could I ever forget them. I walked every nursery and had all the sandwiches on their menus. Then I realised that I felt better if I walked outside, I'd always had a love of trees and nature and found a comfort in the forests and then I realised if I was to survive my mental state then I had to give up everything that stood for my old life, and step forward in to a new way of living.

The night air rushes into the croft as I open the door and step out into the night, I trip over something on the doorstep and kick it onto the grass, my torch is in my coat pocket and soon I begin to search the tufts for the hard object. All I can find is a pile of pebbles, when I pick them up, I realise they all have holes in and are threaded onto a rough piece of string. I know what these are, they are hag stones depending on what you believe in, they can be unlucky or lucky. I hang them by the door on a strong piece of ivy that has secured itself between the cracks in the stone. I am a little curious as to who put them on the step and to the reasons why. I reach the campervan and finally fish out the carrier bag with the catalogues in. I have a good look around the property, perhaps the odd girl has put the stones there, I just wish she would stop and talk for a moment, I'd really like to know where she disappeared to the other day, I could have sworn she went into the croft. I must remember when I next see Betty, at the farm shop, to ask if she knows who she could possibly be.

The seed catalogues are a delight to read and before long I have a long list of plants I want to grow. Without a greenhouse to start them off in I'm not sure how many I can raise on the window-sills. I start another list of vegetables that I can put straight into the soil. I am quite impressed with the amount I can try and grow, also there are masses of herbs and flowers that I can start off indoors and then plant outside in the spring. I also read that I can make a cold frame for the delicate veg that will need to be sheltered, I add more to the ever-growing list, tomorrow when I can get a signal, I will order all the things I need, also I will ask Tom if he can give me any advice on how to make a start. after all he's been growing fruit and veg for years at the farm.

We are so near to Christmas and I have to decide soon if I am going to send greeting cards, my inner self does not want anything to do with this time of year that has no interest for me whatsoever, last year I hardly remember it and bumbled through it still unable to function in the celebrating world. Christmas used to be such a family time of year and over time family members aged unnoticed and then they moved on to other worlds and suddenly you are the only one at the Christmas table the last one standing you could say. This year I still miss my family so much but am trying hard to remember, shall I say it, 'The Good Times.' Sometimes the good times make you weep as much as the bad times, I am thank-full for so many happy memories.

I think of all the things that stand for a child's Christmas, firstly your parents and a warm and loving home which I always had as a child. I can sit back now and close my eyes and see myself in bed on Christmas morning and feel the excitement of knowing Santa Claus had been and there at the bottom of the bed was a pillow case brimming with presents wrapped in brightly coloured paper and silver sticky tape. Cherished presents that grew up with me are now precious keepsakes, my treasured teddy bear that is now so threadbare, a small silver identity bracelet and a musical Jewellery box with a dancing ballerina are stored safely in the loft back at home. So simple then and yet we are so lucky now.

With my mind full of grandmas strange figgy pudding and humorous memories of grandad eating the plastic robin off the Christmas cake and awful cracker jokes that we all laughed at I drift off into a dream filled nap of roaring log fires, sing-a-longs with everyone singing different words, I sleep well into the night all my thoughts about Christmas played on my mind and I am lost in another dream, so real, that I am so surprised when I wake up in the early hours and find myself in this strange cottage. Perhaps not so much a dream as a recollection of the last Christmas we all had together something I thought I had erased from my mind; it seems it was just waiting in the background to be replayed in one of my weak moments.

I am in the kitchen in the old house, peeling sprouts, at the sink. There is a happy aroma of roast turkey and stuffing swirling through the house. The tree in the lounge is lit by a thousand candle lights and there is a warm glow from the fire. Under the tree are the presents I carefully chose for Luca and my mother. It is a week before Christmas and as we always go away for Christmas day, I cook an early meal for my mother who lives on her own. Luca as usual has gone to pick her up. I have found a cd of carols from the choir of Christchurch and they are playing softly in the background. Outside the rain of earlier has turned to sleet and it's starting to look a little festive. Mother will stay for a few days then we will drop her back home on our way to the airport. I really don't notice the time until the timer rings to tell me the turkey is cooked. Usually, Luca is here to lift it out of the oven. At first, I am not to bothered as he has been known to bring Mum back by the scenic route to give her a nice ride into the countryside. And then I have this feeling of foreboding that paralyses me and my dream becomes a nightmare, I wake up stiff and cold still in the dream. How could all that sadness happen and yet the world goes on and mine has stopped. I uncurl my bones and pull out the sofa bed. I nestle into my duvet; how could I sleep so well sitting up and yet now I'm stretched out in bed my eyes are wide awake and my body wants to get up and walk. I fidget about for a little longer and then give up every thought of getting to sleep, my bare feet hit the freezing cold flagstones and I rummage around trying to find my socks. I pull on my trousers over my pyjamas and find a warm sweater. Outside the sky is cloudless and just from the window I can see a million stars filling the universe, the waxing moon is bright and illuminating the countryside with a faint blue light which shines onto the sea, far down on the sands a movement catches my eye, a group of perhaps half a dozen people are moving around, a shiver runs down my spine, they are all huddled together, three of them are holding flaming torches the black smoke curling away into the clear night. I wish I had unpacked my binoculars. The men turn and start to walk up the beach, I have seen these people before, they were here the first night I arrived. I check I have locked the door and wait for them to pass the cottage, silence, nothing, they would have to walk past here there was no other way from the beach unless you climbed over the rocks. I was wide awake but not sure what I had just seen. Perhaps they were some sort of heritage group re-enacting some old tradition, some of these islands are steeped in history and strange traditions. If I am going to stay here there is a lot I must learn about, that's another question on the list for the Grovers.

After a restless night full of troubled dreams, I'm up early enough to catch the most amazing sunrise, bravely I throw open a window to let in the icy cold breeze and to listen to the songs of the first shorebirds to arrive. Already I have learnt so much about the island wildlife, I love the haunting call of the Curlew which is called a song of grief, and at sunset the way the Turnstones actually do turnstones, also that the wind never stops rushing past, it is either breezy or a relentless gale. The wet sand has many tiny feet splashing around looking for their breakfast. Dozens of birds fly in and pick a feeding place, they seem unaware of the drop in the temperature, there is ice in the air and if the clouds build up, I would not be surprised to see a snow shower. The log store had a pile of earth at the back and I discovered it was peat blocks, I've wedged a whole one into the burner it instantly quelled the bright orange flames and now through the glass door I can see just a grey spiral of steam. The room has quickly cooled down since I opened the window and just to add to the freezing temperature the gas boilers ignition won't light, I wash just the bits you can see with cold water even the soap doesn't want to work today, I dry myself with one of the absorbent camping towels I brought with me and dress quickly.

After trying to boil a kettle I realise the gas has run out, somewhere there are instructions on how to switch the bottles over, I search through the dresser drawers nothing, in the kitchen I find the folder under a tray piled with tea-cloths. The file contains instructions for all the equipment and a long itinerary of all the contents and a harsh warning that I will be charged for all breakages. It assures me that the spanner for changing the gas bottle will be found hanging on a hook inside the larder and sure enough it wasn't. I find the car keys and brave the icy blast, my tool box is stored under the back-bench seat along with many useful things I might need, I find the box and an adjustable spanner, the gas bottles are situated in a wooden box just outside the kitchen window, nothing in the folder said I also need a key for the padlock on the box, I leave the spanner on the top of the box and go back around to the front door. The croft keyring is in the kitchen, wisely I put my warm coat on before I go back outside, I close the front door, hoping to keep the little bit of warmth in, as I step outside, I think I can feel a little sleet in the harsh wind. Back at the gas box the spanner is nowhere to be found, I know where I left it, but it doesn't matter how long I stare at the empty place it has disappeared. I keep cool and refuse to fill my mind with any further drama, off I go to the van again to get another spanner, absolute madness, I shake my head in disbelief there inside on the bench seat is the spanner. 'One of us is crazy,' I say to myself, often I think everyone has two people inside them, the sensible law-abiding citizen and stalwart of the adult community, who can be relied on and then the other one the daft unreliable bumbling childish drama queen. I am not sure who I am today but have a really good idea.

With a few cuss words I manage to change the gas bottle over and am pleased to hear the hiss of the butane and watch the blue blazing ring under the kettle. The early start I intended has passed, not that I really have a time scale, I purposely left all watches and clocks back at home. Time is free here, no rules to do anything, I eat when I like and what I like, I could have breakfast at supper time or dinner first thing, I walk in the day or at night, complete freedom nothing to confine me.

I make a cup of lemon and ginger tea and toast the last crust of bread, this afternoon if I don't get distracted, I will visit the farm shop for a few supplies and ask about the girl and the men on the beach last night, which in the true light of day I am not sure whether they were real or not. Perhaps I'll just ask about the girl, I don't want to give them the impression that I am mad. One ghost at a time, that's what I believe.

The wind is relentless and the van rocks when it's gusty blast hits it broad-side, the hills are magnificent and so vividly green against the azure blue sky, the scenery is so beautiful it is hard to put into words. I slow down and stop, far on the hill I can see what I thought were horses but as I have come closer, I realise they are red deer, magnificent creatures tall with great branches of antlers on their heads, they are grazing amongst the faded heather, not many, perhaps five at the most. I could sit all day and watch and wait for wildlife, but not today. I move on and drive through the moorland and soon come across the Farm shop nestled in a layby at the bottom of the driveway to Weathercote Farm. I notice a strong metal gate across the drive is secured with a padlock, so he really doesn't want visitors.

The shop is deceiving, from the outside it appears to be a wooden shed with a few vegetable boxes outside, inside it is a pandoras box of surprises, fresh hens or beautiful blue duck eggs, local caught fish and seafood, a small selection of fruit, local bakery bread of various types. And there is also local grown meat and vacuum packs of cold ham, brawn and smoked venison. Mrs. Grover comes to serve me an recommends the duck and orange pate that she has just made, she points to small brown earthenware bowls with olives and fresh orange slices covering the delicious mess, I really should have thought before I nodded and then continued to fill my basket with nothing basic or really needed. Mrs. Grover's eyes became pound signs as I added crackers and chutney, olives, bread sticks, three different cheeses, pickled onions which I'm not particularly keen on and then all the things I really came in for.

I paid her and she kindly packed the provision in a cardboard box. I asked her, did she know of a young girl who waits up on the rocks and walks by the beach, at first, she hesitated and looked away from me, but I pursued the matter and told her I thought the poor girl needed help as she appeared distraught. She changed her mood and cautiously said she must be staying somewhere nearby, perhaps she drives to the beach, she said it was best not to get involved with the locals as some might take offence to my interference, as I was a visitor with no knowledge of the island or the people. I took it that somehow, I had been rebuked for caring.

Well, I left out of pocket and none the wiser to the identity of the girl. The drive back was bumpy and I was glad to park the van and take my box of goodies indoors. The light was so amazing that I donned my walking gear and set off for the shoreline, the tide was out and I could see a path around the bay, as soon as I left the exposure of the wind blowing off of the ocean it seemed a little warmer.

The sand and shell path wound around the bay and was littered with great swathes of gleaming wet seaweed attached tightly to large pebbles. When I was a child, I would trail ribbons of kelp back home and hang it in the garden as my Grandfather said you could forecast the weather by the feel of it, when it was dry, the sun would shine and when wet it was going to rain, no magic really all common sense when you're an adult. I am so tempted, so I select a piece I can handle and pull it along behind me. I turn around as I can hear a thumping sound and I am a little surprised to see a horse and rider come into view galloping at great speed along the water's edge, the rider, a man has his head down and pushes the horse on, the horse a beautiful chestnut moves easily, his long dark brown mane floating in the air as he thunders across the beach, in seconds they have reached the headland and disappeared from my view. Riding like that must be quite exhilarating, I can ride but haven't tried it for a long time, I suppose there must be riding stables here somewhere, it's got to be a lot easier than driving, some of the roads are for horses or walkers only. As I reach the small rocky headland, I cannot help but notice the amount of noise coming from the birds, gulls of some sort, the whole rock face is a home for these noisy white birds that seem to be having a permanent argument with each other, the rocks are splattered with white and grey poo, making it look like an abstract piece of artwork, I move away as I don't want them to christen my new coat just yet. As I turn the corner the anger of the North wind hits my face and nearly knocks me over, I move quickly back into the lee of the bay and retrace my footsteps. I step over rock pools that are whole worlds to the crab's shrimps and shellfish that live in them, I spend a little time just searching through the clear water amazed how many creatures there are. The gulls had been busy and the beach is decorated with colourful empty shells, I fill my pockets with souvenirs intending to make some sort of collage with them, then I find another treasure to carry back, beautiful dull washed out drift wood, all in a heap on the sand, I fill my pockets and imagine all that I can make with it, I keep close to the rock wall and am pleased to discover small caves set far into the rocks, I must have missed them when I walked past earlier, they are quite high and wide and presume they are tunnelled under the hillside. I suppose the fishermen might have used them a long time ago, they look as though you could almost live in one, mind you I'm not sure about high tides when they would be flooded. The walk is turning out to be far more interesting than I first thought, my mind is a lot more settled than when I first left the croft. I think Luca would have loved this place, perhaps not the solitude as he was a people person and loved company, but he would have loved the sea and the views. Such a shame we were not able to share the whole of our life together, I must admit I never ever thought that our lives would change so tragically, I took it all for granted. I remind myself when I am in the, 'Sorry me place', that it is okay and normal to still feel the grief and to become so overwhelmed by the tragedy, that it feels like it happened only yesterday. Grief is bad enough but add shock to it and it becomes unbelievable, everything takes time and there are no rules to how long, you live with it, it's real, it did happen, you have to listen to your own advice, however long it takes, no-one can do this for you or advise you how to grieve and when to stop loving, if ever.

I have the cold wind behind me and the sky has changed to various shades of grey, the lower clouds fleet across the horizon and build up threatening rain. Like a child with pockets full of treasures I retrace my footsteps, but as I look down, I realise these are not just my footsteps, there are other sets beside mine, I think of the girl, but these are a men's size feet, an uncomfortable feeling waves over me as the footprints stop, and then nothing. I search all around me as to where the person could have gone without leaving a mark in the wet sand, perhaps they climbed the rocks or as I suspect went into one of the caves. I carry on back to the croft and make it to the door as the grey sky flashes and bangs and sends down a hailstorm, I leave the large pieces of driftwood and seaweed by the front door and make a note to string up the kelp tomorrow. Darkness has come early as the low clouds shroud the hilltops and close in the countryside. I unpack my pockets and place all the sandy shells along the windowsills, I have an empty jar and put the feathers and small pieces of driftwood in it, a rather nice collection from an enjoyable afternoon.

I am ready for a mince pie, one of Mrs. Grover specials, she assures me she makes the best pastry on the island and people travel miles for her mince pies and Christmas puddings, these pies are an exception to my total ban on anything festive, even though I did have my eyes on a few fine sprigs of Holly, which was absolutely covered in bright red berries. I might succumb to have a jam jar on the dresser of Holly and a few strands of ivy from around the door. I want

Christmas day to be the same as every other day and hope it passes quickly, I find it hard to celebrate these times without loved ones and just want to ignore it, one day it might change but not yet it's too early. I'll know when I'm ready.

The rain outside has turned to a cold icy sleet and the croft becomes dark and drafty, as the cruel north wind forgets its manners and enters the room, through the ill-fitting windows and old front door. I rake the dying embers of the fire and open the glass door, to let the heat out into the freezing room. I sit down with a fresh coffee and a directory of island birds and wildlife; I discover that the angry gulls on the rock face were Kittiwakes and then I become thoroughly engrossed into the book and make a note as to what I can expect to find on the island. I write todays findings in my journal and a brief description of my day especially the footsteps on the beach and my extravagant and elaborate items I bought at the farm shop.

I am so pleasantly full to the gunnels with delicious mince pies and am just about ready to doze when I hear the rumbling of horse's hooves again, this time they are a lot nearer and coming up the beach, I look out just as the rider stops opposite the front door. It is quite dark outside and I find it difficult to see who it is, but just by looking at the arrogant way the man is sitting and staring it's the same man who chased me to give back my purse. I don't feel frightened or menaced by him in any way only curious as to why he's out in such weather and where does he come from. He moves around to the side of the garden and seems to pay attention to the patch I have roughly dug, then it occurs to me, perhaps this man younger than I had thought could be the owner of this croft if not, he's certainly nosey. I can't bear it any longer and open the front door and am instantly blasted by the wind. He sees the light from the door and steers the horse back around to the front gate. I step outside and walk towards him; he's saying something to me but the wind snatches his words away. He shakes his head and roughly pulls the horses head around and gallops off into the night. I am sure this isn't the last I'll hear from this man. It takes quite an effort to close the door, when the squally wind is so determined to push its way in.

MEMORIES ARE A SPECIAL GIFT NEVER TO BE LOST.

Eventually when I finally dropped off last night, I was taken into a series of dreams that this morning has, left me happy and also sad. Most of my dreams are made up of strange uncomfortable weird events, but last night it was the first time since I lost Luca that I felt we had met again. The details I remember so clearly, it was all so real as if we existed in another dimension, slipping in and out of reality. Luca was waiting for me in the car, it was raining, he had driven out of his way to pick me up so I didn't get wet waiting for the bus. I was so pleased to see him and happily got into the car. I said to him I thought he had left me and I would never see him again. His laughter was so real, 'What ever made you say that,' he asked, and gripped my hand in assurance. In my dream he was so alive, I could smell his warm skin that I knew so well and see his forget-me-not blue eye. In the car, I could hear his favourite c.d playing gently in the back-ground, a broad smile lit his face as he turned to look at me, we stopped at the traffic lights that I knew so well. Our house was just around the next corner, we drew up outside, everything looked quite normal, I stepped out of the car expecting Luca to follow, but he stayed in the driving seat, I opened the passenger door and said, 'We are home are you coming in,' he laughed and shook his head, 'No I'm not.' 'Why,' I asked, 'Because I don't have to, It's not my home anymore.' He drove off. In my sleep part of my brain was trying to say,' This is a dream and not real,' but I was enjoying the moment so much. I woke with the familiar soft warm tears washing my face. This was the first time I really felt I had met Luca since his death and it made me feel sad but so happy, I think Luca was dream hopping when he and I shared a memory, him in another world and me in mine.

Today I'm going to spend the whole day walking on the island. It is Christmas day and I can honestly say that this is the hardest of all days. I feel nothing but overwhelming sadness, I am so glad that I am here far away from all the reminders that are woven into the exterior of my house back in the great capital. Some memories are precious and comforting and I hope I never ever forget them, but others are not welcome and it is a constant battle to push them away.

Of course, the wind as usual is relentless and I feel like an Everest climber as I hitch my rucksack on my back and push myself out of the door. Everything outside is totally unaware of me and anything about me. The world is such a vast place and it is completely oblivious of us, it turns and turns evolves through all the ages and we are just ants living on its crust, actually we mean nothing in the scheme of things. The universe has the power to let us live or die, we think we rule the world, I think not, there are much greater forces than mere man who pollutes his own space and fails to live with each other, we are still primitive.

I packed most of my rucksack last night and made my picnic, so I could make an early start. I now have a map of the island wrapped in a transparent folder it hangs around my neck so I can't lose it. The wind is quite forceful as I head up the hill towards the rocks, there is a little sleet in the icy wind, my new clothes are certainly working I am quite toasty. I stop for a few minutes to look back at the bay, the grey clouds reflect in the water, only a few sea birds on the beach today. In front of me the path is littered with green stones moulded with amazing mosses resembling flocked fabric. Ahead the ruins of the small chapel appear, again the stone is painted by nature, mosses and yellow lichens have permeated the cracks and fissures of the aged relic. The colours of the countryside are quite vibrant against the grey clouds, a few scraggy gorse bushes are either blooming early or really late, they are splashed with small pods of bright yellow, these windswept bushes make a perfect hiding place the hares and rabbits which graze here. The shades up here are an ever-changing pallet, rocks have taken on a purple hue and the grassy path has changed to loose stone, my boots grip really well, overhead the crazy Kittiwakes twist, turn and scream with delight as they soar in the ever-increasing wind. As the temperature drastically drops the sleet starts to turn to snow and I stop walking, just to savour the welcome winter weather, years ago in my other life I would wish for a white Christmas just to get the atmosphere, strange how that happens, eventually I get my wish and it's not really what I want. I peer through the snow and can just about see the croft way down at the bottom of the hill, I've climbed quite a way up and am eager to push on.

As I leave the ruins, I come upon a small ancient burial ground, over time the graves have sunk and slipped ungraciously into the earth, the stone covers have fractured and nature has taken advantage and planted small seedlings into the cracks. Inscriptions once readable have been long forgotten, eroded by age and are intelligible. I wonder who these people were, to have been buried so high on this hill in such a beautiful place. I am reluctant to leave this peaceful moment and promise myself to spend more time up here in the future. The weather now is typical winter, the wind is driving the snow into small drifts, filling the crooks and crevices of the rocks. I feel like I'm walking through the iced frosting on a Christmas cake and cannot believe how amazing it is. I have no idea where I am as I have never walked this far before, I know the island is not that big and the worst thing that could happen would be I could fall off.

In front of me a hare scratches in the soft snow and rushes for cover as I approach, I crunch through the heather and shelter in a small group of rocks surrounded by rough bushes. I find my flask and pour a small cup of black coffee, the steam spirals up into the icy air, it tastes like nectar and quickly cools in the cold air, I don't really feel that hungry but, decide to eat now as I don't want to stop again for a while. The banana right at the bottom of my rucksack, feels frozen and I have to remove my gloves to peel the stiff skin, so quickly my fingers become quite numb with the cold, the banana lolly takes quite a bit of chewing and am pleased when it has finally been eaten.

This morning I actually managed to make a filling breakfast, in true Scottish style I actually cooked a large copper saucepan, brimming with real porridge oats, the wooden spoon insisted on standing to attention in the middle of the glutinous mess. I persevered with it and after a good helping, I could hardly bend down to put my shoes on, I hoped the weight of it would not impair my long trek. I remind myself I have an extremely congealed pan to clean when I get back.

I am fully refreshed and leave the shelter and move on, visibility has deteriorated and all I can see through the veil of fine snow is a group of horses, they are ignoring the weather and grazing on the tufts of grass that poke through the snow. To my right I can see a drop so gather that I am walking along the cliff top. As I near the edge a flurry of birds rise up, squabble noisily in mid-air and drop back down from view, they seem annoyed by my presence and I move back from them. A couple decide I have not given them enough space and swoop quite close to my head. I feel the draft from their fluttering and liken it to the breeze from an angel's wings, not that I have ever felt it, but I am sure it would feel like that.

I have reached the top of the world and each way I look is just nothing except a blizzard of icy particles that ping off my red cheeks. I suddenly stop walking and pause; I try to get my bearings. No idea which way to go next, after my detour to the edge of the cliff I turned back or did I? did I go east or west or one of the others? I can't even see the horses. Oh well, it really does not concern me that I have no idea where I am, and at this moment it really doesn't matter, I am free from everything up here, I am nothing but part of nature, I bite my lip to stop the threat of screaming at the world, as at last there is some comfort to the constant draining grief, I wish I could be a bird flying high in the air on the thermals with no idea of how complicated humans lives are, or a hare eating, running, oblivious to anything other than the moment, with this incredible island as his home, no walls to contain him and nothing material in his life, how do they survive without all the chattels and complications we create for ourselves. Recently I have pondered on the thought that the more technology we have the more we become impatient, dissatisfied and always wanting and becoming isolated from each other, forming relationships with social media and all the trappings of technology that goes with it. I was the biggest culprit before my life was stripped down to the bone. I have altered my priorities, its people that matter and feelings, something we only realise when it is too late.

I don't know how long it will take me to get used to being this new person, but I feel I am heading forward in the right direction. I have realised that you cannot go back and nothing can ever be the same again, that's all there was of that part of my past life, it's over, nothing is permanent and I am starting another stage with a blank journal and am ready to fill it.

I keep moving, every so often the snow turns to sleet and I can see through it, the sea is still to the right of me. It is a miraculous sight to be up so high and look down on the ocean, the colours are a mixture of grey wild water and white frothy foam, rolling endlessly from coast to coast on a relentless passage. The snow has drifted in some parts, covering the grass and rocks with a soft icing of crystals, all around me the land is so perfect, the snow has made all the hillside the same colour and it is fresh and untouched by man, just the occasional footprint of a bird. I listen, no sound except the soft patter of snow flakes, even the noisy cliff birds have settled down tucked in the many crevices of the rock face. I was hoping to see the comical puffins but even they are hiding from the weather.

As I make my way up the next stage of the hill the walk seems a little bit harder and noticeably colder, the snow is deeper the higher I go. I have to lean forward as the path winds around the headland, it is narrowing as it changes direction and rolls out into a precarious track. I take my time and walk cautiously trying not to look down at my fate if I slip. The wind rips at my hood and frozen beads blind me, I feel the rock wall for something to hold onto, I stop abruptly as I realise this direction cannot possibly be the route I planned, I must have lost concentration and made a silly mistake, somehow, I have taken the wrong path and am now precariously perched on a thin strip of ice-covered rock. My legs are trembling as I try to turn around and retrace my footsteps but the ledge is so narrow and I can't see what's behind me. My coat seems extra warm and really heavy and my muscles have become stiff and rigid. The roosting birds that I disturbed, mock me with their shrill calls, at this moment I wish I could fly. I push myself inward against the rock wall and try to remove my gloves so

I can get a grip, this is not how I planned to exit this world, I want it to be a lot more exciting than this. I am not one to pray or pretend to, but at this moment I resort to asking for help, I know from past experience that when you pray and plea, there is no-one to hear you, or answer. I ask Luca, if you can hear me, I am stuck here on this cliff and I don't know what to do. As always when I say his name I am overwhelmed with the reality of my loss. My heart sinks, the grey clouds that haunt me fill my body with lead, I feel like I have been fighting a battle to survive on my own and I am really just slowly losing.

The wind whistles around me oblivious of my predicament, what in heavens name possessed me, an absolute novice at hiking or even walking to take on such an expedition, I really should have paid more attention to my map instead of stupidly putting myself in this dangerous situation. Carefully I shuffle my feet backwards and feel for some sort of grip on the snow-covered surface, the wind pushes me and I cling to a small tree stump that has rooted between the rocks, teardrops run freely and turn to ice as they drop onto my coat. My gloveless hands are numb and painful, the tough jagged rocks have torn the flesh on my fingers and fresh blood stains the snowy surface. My stiff legs shuffle slowly sideways and inch by inch I am retracing my fateful steps. Time seems to stand still, the wind batters me and inflates the hood on my coat, ripping it from my head, the icy blast roars in my ears and deadens any other sound. As I turn away from the blast I gasp as I feel a hand on my shoulder, I can't turn to look, the grip tightens and pulls me. Above the noisy gale a man's voice is shouting at me, 'It's Okay I've got you, keep stepping backwards.'

My whole body is trembling as I trust the voice and edge my way towards him. In a very blurred moment, I am back on safe ground and collapse in a heap into the snow, I am so eager to see who my rescuer is, he is dressed in a navy-blue parker jacket and well equipped for the bad weather. Dark glasses mask his eyes, he stoops down in front of me. 'Are you alright, whatever possessed you to go out on the cliff in this weather, lucky I was out walking.' I muttered an apology and my grateful thanks for the second time to this man and then slowly standing up I added, 'I am Alice, I live in the croft at the bottom of the hill,' he towered above me. 'I know who you are, I am Simon Blake of Weathercote Farm and I own the croft. Now if you are okay, I'd rather get on with my walk. And, by the way, next time be more careful where you walk, you townies are all the same you don't understand the dangers of this place,' and then added, 'Merry Christmas,' as he disappeared into the blizzard.

It took me quite a while to gather myself together and I was still physically shaken when I decided to discontinue my journey and return home. In my troubled mind I wondered if Luca had sent me the help and if so, perhaps next time could it be someone not quite so condescending, I feel an absolute idiot.

As I trudged down the hill my body felt like a lump of lead, the snow was getting heavier, settling and covering the whole landscape, breathtakingly beautiful but deadly. I was glad to see the croft, but felt quite troubled. Before I went inside, I gathered an armful of logs and stacked them at the front door whilst I searched for the key. My sore fingers delved inside all the pockets, I pulled everything out onto the step and could not believe I had lost the key. I pushed the door hoping by some miracle I hadn't locked it and to my surprise it opened easily, I was so relieved I stepped inside and hurriedly closed the door against all the wind and snow and embarrassing moments.

As I filled the kettle, I am suddenly startled, as I notice a figure standing in the snow not far from the gate, that damned girl is there looking out to sea, she has no coat on and must be freezing, I grab my coat from the back of the door and rush outside. She stands unmoving, as I approach her, she turns her head to face me and my heart freezes as she opens her mouth to talk but, the words are silent and lost in the wind. Her startling blue eyes plead with me. She says the words over and over again, I concentrate really hard and I read her lips, 'Help me, please, please help me.' My blood runs cold, I want to help her. I ask her to come inside and warm up and tell me how I can help. She looks through me and not at me. I notice beneath her dress she seems a lot thinner than the last time I saw her and her clothes are not quite as clean as before, she has certainly deteriorated. I am really concerned for her well-being and feel she really needs some help. I step forward and attempt to put my coat over her shoulders she steps away from me and almost glides away, it is then that I notice she leaves no footprints in the snow, I move away not sure what is happening. A voice behind me causes me to turn around, my landlord has finished his walk and had noticed that I was still out in the snow and thought to enquire what I was doing. I ask him did he see the girl I was talking to and did he know who she was, as I thought she was in some sort of trouble. He seemed quite serious and assured me, in no uncertain terms that, coming down the hill he could see that I was on my own and was talking to myself. He then suggested I get indoors in the warm as the cold had a strange way of affecting some people who were not accustom to it. Before I could explain what had been really happening, he had turned away from me and all I could see was the back of this arrogant man leaving, ignoring everything I said.

The rest of my Christmas day was spent trying to make sense of the whole blessed day.

YOUR BELIEFS ARE YOUR PROPERTY.

I am beginning to feel me or the croft is haunted. After the girl's visit I have had quite a few odd things happen. I am only too glad that the dark evenings are drawing out and we have now reached the halfway mark of the winter, the pagan festival of Imbolc, when light is starting to come back to the world. I can certainly see a slight touch of growth on some of the trees in the orchard.

I am eager to continue with clearing a patch of garden for my vegetables. Today the weather is a little milder not warmer just not so freezing. The wind has changed from the cruel north to the south, so blows slightly off the land and is much kinder.

In January I sent for some seeds, I really did get carried away and was surprised when I picked up the parcel from the post office. Tom has offered to bring me a few bags of well-rotted horse manure from the farm, I made him laugh when I said if it was from his employer's horses it was nearly royal poo and my seeds were sure to grow well. Tom and his wife are really nice people and never ask any questions about why I am here, they leave me well alone unless I ask them for help. I tried to talk to them about the croft being haunted and they laughed and said all old buildings rattle and creak and as for the girl she must live somewhere nearby. I think they are humouring me and think I am a little mad and treat me kindly.

So many nights I am woken by tapping in the attic and horrible shouting on the wind, I can also hear someone sobbing and then there is the knocking at my door and the group of men tramping past and the lanterns and torches on the cliffs. Such a busy place in the middle of nowhere. I am glad that I have bought ear-plugs with me, something that I needed in London a city that doesn't sleep, even at night the streets are noisy with taxis and street cleaners.

The earth is not as sticky as the last time I tried to dig. Like a true gardener I have pegged out the boundary with string and have tried to cut a straight edge around it. I envisage beautiful rows of fresh vegetables and salad. My boots are getting heavy with encrusted mud and I rest for a moment and scrape them, I can hear a car engine approaching, quite a rarity, Tom's Land rover comes into view, I wave before I realise that Tom is not the driver. My heart sinks as Simon Blake pulls up outside. He unloads two bags of manure and stands them against the wall. I find it difficult to be nice so I settle for well mannered. I thank him and ask him how much I owe him. He says Tom will settle it with me. And then of course as all arrogant people, he again takes the wind out of my fragile sails and tells me, that he would prefer it if I had asked him first about digging up the garden, and would I please not destroy the ancient stone wall to edge the veg patch with. My happy mood drops into my boots and I have to remind myself that he is my landlord, but then my ego steps in and I remind him in no uncertain terms he is taking my hard-earned money for rental on this old, cold, damp haunted property that is equipped from the middle ages and what right did he have to be so rude to me all the time. And I think I most probably mentioned the word motherless again. He just stands there looking at me. I say to him, 'If you want me to leave just say so and I'll go, I didn't come here to cause trouble in fact the opposite. I was pleased when your agent said you were a recluse and I wouldn't see you,' and then I added, 'Just go and write your blessed book or draw your damn pictures but get out of my space.'

I am so ready to give this lark up as a bad job, peace is not something I have had since I came here, I think that the idea was good but I chose the wrong place. In temper I kick off my boots and fling them out into the mud patch and slam the rotten front door hoping it will come off its hinges and fall into a heap of sawdust. I don't wait to see him leave. I don't really know what I want, but I know what I don't want is anyone being unkind or telling me off. At first when they died, I couldn't function normally as there was nothing left that was stable, no anchor, slowly I have had to find me, and forge a new life without my family. I have kept myself at a distance from people and confrontation and am feeling this man is intruding into my space, not kindly but over petty things that are not important when you have experienced the serious side of life.

I spend the next few hours attempting to connect to the internet, trying to find a new place to hide. The internet is so annoying and adds to my frustrations. I give up and decide to go into the village and ask at the post office if they know of anywhere else to rent. I want to stay on the island but not here. The journey through the hills back to the village seems to take forever, I hardly take any notice of the countryside around me and automatically drive, everything feels uncomfortable again. It is late afternoon and the lights are on in all the shops. I park in the square and walk the short distance to the post office. The postmistress is surprised when I ask her about property to rent and wants to know the reason why I want to leave the croft. I change the subject and bypass her nosey-ness and ask her to let me know if she hears of anything. I also added I would be grateful if she kept it to herself, she nodded in agreement but I suspected that the village grapevine started at the post office.

The spade looks as though it has been abandoned in the centre of the garden, at the moment I think I have lost enthusiasm for gardening. I still haven't, found the door key and let myself in using the spare, somewhere upon the hill in the snow is my key, hopefully one of the walkers will find it.

The sunset this evening is like my mood, dull and lacks some of the colours of late. The sea is still and reflects the pallid sky. I walk down to the shoreline and can just about see the edge of the sea; it is so far out that great sandbanks have been exposed. I take off my shoes and walk barefoot, the wet sand is comforting, cool water seeps through my toes. Shore birds take little notice of me as I silently pass by them, I walk, but the sea gets no nearer. Behind me the weak sunset hardly lights the croft windows, oddly enough there is a flickering light shining from the small skylight window in the roof, after a few minutes it goes dark. This place is full of strange phenomena's apparently, this is also the perfect spot to see the aurora borealis another weird and wonderful event but, only when the conditions are right. The night clouds roll in and the dim sun slowly sets, reluctantly I turn away from the sea and walk back to the beach. Somewhere a single curlew calls and clouds of lapwings flee inland to roost for the night. Stars are starting to appear in the dusky sky, amazing to think they are always up there night and day, but we need darkness to see their light. In my deepest moments I have tried to analyse the meaning of man's existence and it baffles me to the point that I become overwhelmed with all the theories and now I am so confused that I settle for the explanation that, this is all such a marvellous miracle and the answers to its creation are not in this world, it is all so much greater than we will ever understand. We are just here to play our part and keep the world populated. I have learnt the only way is to live for this moment, yesterday was history and just a memory, tomorrow never ever comes, it is always, today. We have choices on how we spend our given time between life and death and must leave with no regrets, which are really just mistakes of the past, at the time they were not mistakes and we did what was best. Regrets come sometime later when you think you might have got it wrong.

I have walked off my grumpiness It's amazing what nature and fresh air can do. I continue without my shoes as my feet are encrusted with sand and shell dust, the night air is pleasant and I spend a little longer outside listening to nature's night-time lullaby. Somewhere an owl calls for a mate and far up the hill the dark shadows of the deer move, silently grazing.

The first thing I notice when I reach the croft is that there is a key already in the lock, I wonder whoever found it, and more worrying how did they know it was mine. I sigh with despair, yet another mystery. I inspect the rooms, everything is alright, nothing has been touched. I'm too awake to go to sleep and have another go at reading one of the books from the shelf. It is so frayed and delicate, it's an account of the Blake family tree and all the occupiers of Weathercote Farm dating back hundreds of years. The family appeared once to be the only landowners on the island but gradually sold off land and property over the years, their main produce was sheep, employing many workers. The account of the family and their fortunes stop in 1850, my eyes have become heavy trying to read in such dim light and even though I want to read further about the mysterious disappearance of Alice Blake, daughter of the landowner I wearily close the heavy book and turn off the lamp.

Thank goodness Christmas has passed and I managed to avoid New Year's Eve, it was really kind of Betty and Tom to ask me to their house for drinks, I think they understood when I declined., I didn't go into any detail, I just said thank you, but no. I was surprised when they came to visit, they delivered a rotovator to the croft, sent from their employer, he thought it might make digging over the garden a bit easier, Tom insisted on demonstrating how to drive it and ended up turning over the whole plot, whilst I made Betty coffee. I was a little suspicious as to the reason that the arrogant man had changed his mind about me growing veg. Betty tried to ask about my family and I still wasn't ready to discuss my private life with anyone here. Here I am just Alice from London.

Today I am expecting the delivery of my bee hives, they are coming from the mainland, and I think I have found someone on one of the other islands who can supply me with the bees later in the year. I think the bees will be happy here; I am assured in the summer the area is covered in heather and wild flowers. It looks like I am to stay here a bit longer than I want to. I did not have one single reply to my card in the post office. All the empty crofts are either owned by Simon Blake or purely seasonal rentals.

I have found a perfect patch for the hives in the orchard, against the wall, the area seems to be devoid of any vegetation whatsoever and only needs levelling which will take no time at all.

The hills look dark today and the snow of Christmas has left a few faint traces but has mainly thawed. A few walkers passed this morning and asked if I sold drinks and refreshments, I offered them water to fill their bottles with and thought this could be something to think about for the future. I suppose I would have to ask permission from my landlord, perhaps I'll give that idea a miss, even-though I really want to make and sell honey and preserves eventually. I have toyed with the thought that I could possibly sell the house in London and buy here and then I wouldn't be beholding to anyone. I'll give it a year and see how it goes; I am so nervous of making rash decisions I could live to regret. I have to learn to trust my instinct, it is all so hard now, before there was always two of us to decide on everything.

I can hear the truck rumbling down the road, long before I can see it. A really jolly driver carries the hives into the orchard, he laughs as I tell him my plan to make honey and informs me, his mate Jake, will find me a couple of swarms when I need them and gives me his number. Rob says he was born here in the Shetlands and him and his mate Jake make the hives and lots of other wooden things made out of old pallets, but they don't keep bees anymore as they can be troublesome. He assures me it can be quite easy to keep bees once you've supplied them with the right habitat and if they like their new home they will settle, you just have to keep them happy and well informed as to what is going on, in fact he says the only way really is to talk to them and they will get used to your voice and this will keep them from swarming, but if your angry or really sad don't let them know as they could pick up your mood and buzz off, I laughed at the last statement and thought, what a breath of life he was. He stayed for coffee and invited himself back sometime to see how the hives were settling. I was quite sorry to see him leave and promised to phone him when I was ready for the bees.

The orchard looks quite sad at the moment as the trees are resting. The fruit trees are quite old and gnarled, Tom said he would show me how to prune them, even though they had been neglected for a long time he said they always had a healthy crop, especially the apple trees. I thought it could be good to have a couple of sheep in there if I fenced off the veg patch so they couldn't get in. He laughed and said he would see what he could do.

In one of my boxes, which is still not completely unpacked I found a packet of sachets of dried yeast and a large bag of bread flour. I have tried to make bread in the past and even the birds would not eat it. Luca would say that you could build houses with it. I decide today is the day to start my self-sufficiency, which I know from past experience will not last long. I have a limited selection of baking equipment, but manage to make the mixture and start the strenuous procedure of kneading. I have cleaned the Formica worktop and it will have to do for a pastry board. In the time it took me to knead and prove and knead again I could have driven to the bakery and bought a fresh loaf. I put the brick in the pre-heated oven and use the timer on my phone. An amazing aroma fills the kitchen and wafts into the other room.

I am engrossed in sorting out my seed packets when I am disturbed by the timer on my phone telling me the bread is cooked. I lifted out the incredible sculpture and tipped it out of the tin. At first appearance it looked quite amazing an almost as good as the bakery, this is a first for me. I have bought some goats cheese flavoured with garlic and herbs and fresh salad from Betty. Tom gave me a sample bottle of his own hedgerow wine which, seems a perfect accompaniment for the cheese. The bread knife in the cutlery draw is bendy and really does not want to cut through the bread so I am given to ripping it apart, the bread is still warm and melts the butter which dribbles, making a golden puddle on the plate. I sit at the table in the window and enjoy my lunch. The view never ceases to thrill me, the weather here is so unpredictable and can change so quickly, which is quite alarming when you are out on the hills. I leave

Tom's wine for another day as I suspect it will be quite strong and the day is still young.

The coffee machine splutters and I settle down back at the table, something has changed outside, a thick white mist has rolled off the sea and is swirling up the beach towards the croft. Very quickly the croft is enveloped, I shiver as the temperature drops and the room becomes freezing. I move to look out of the window, through the mist I can see something moving, getting nearer, I strain my eyes to see what it is, I hold my breath as an icy fingers trails down my spine, not a foot from the window, a face suddenly looms at me, I step backwards and trip, my coffee cup sprawls across the table and my chair hits the floor as I step away from the window. I'm not sure what I have just witnessed but, I think it was the girl, she was so thin the bones on her face were showing through her skin and her beautiful eyes were black and sunken, she waved at me with a skeletal hand and I could see her beautiful hair was matted and hanging limply around her emancipated face. I don't know how long I stood looking at her but for the first time I was actually frightened to what I was seeing. I want to go outside and see if I can talk to her, but I am frozen to the spot. A loud banging in the loft distracts me and as I look back, she has gone and the mist is rolling back out to sea.

I try to rationalise what has happened here this afternoon, this very moment, and cannot find a reasonable explanation for the girl's presence and deterioration, if she is human why won't she talk to me. And then it dawns on me, perhaps in the state I am in I am able to cross over in the worlds and see the dead. If so, why can't I see Luca and Mamma. I have an idea that the girl is trying to tell me something and I believe that it has to do with the book I've been reading. If I am honest, I find all this however alarming quite a distraction from the turmoil of thoughts that have been dominating my brain for the last two years, I am frightened by what has just happened, it appears, she is deteriorating each time I see her but I'm inquisitive enough to want to find out more. If I am not mistaken, she is my namesake, Alice, that must be the connection.

After a strong cup of coffee and a check on the locked front door I return to the old book. It was reported that she and her dog were often out all day and sometimes well into the night and often would return to Weathercote farm in the early hours of the morning, she had a passion for sketching wildlife and would wait patiently for hours to see an otter or snow hare, something she had done since a small child, she was fifteen when she failed to return, a shepherd said he had seen her near the fishing croft earlier that afternoon. It was a stormy night and after a long search on the estate and shoreline it was deemed, she and the dog had most probably perished in the stormy sea. There is not much more information about her and the book goes on to mention her parents and other siblings. On the back cover, is handwritten obituaries to some family members and dates they were born and died. Alice's name is not there so, I presume she was never found.

It is well into the night when I put the book away and fall into a troubled sleep, I am dreaming of Luca and Alice and me walking through a forest, the sun is making dappled sunlight through the trees, a dog runs ahead of us and we are all laughing, everyone is alive and healthy, then the beautiful sun is veiled by a cobweb of dark clouds, the once green forest becomes dark and cold, the trees turn into ugly black fingers of decay, as I look at Alice she is a withered old lady with black eye sockets and yellowed bones protruding from her thin flesh. Part of me knows this is not real and is only a dream that has turned into a nightmare, but I cannot wake up from it. Luca has gone from the dream and Alice has collapsed into a pile of ragged clothes, I can barely make out the white daisies on her dress, a loud scratching sound from somewhere above me makes me look up into the black trees, and then I am completely awake, and sitting up in bed, I realise that the horrible scraping noise is coming from the attic above me. I imagine its rats and that they are gnawing through the rafters. I am still shaken from the dream; the noise stops and I make a note to send an e-mail to the agent about the vermin in the roof. I don't mind wildlife but do not want to share with them. It would be quicker to talk to the owner, but I know this is not allowed and besides he's definitely not approachable.

This morning I am washed out and feel I could sleep for a week. This is not turning out as I had expected, I am weighing up how long I am going to be able to put up with the weird things that keep happening. Half-heartedly I pull on my wellies and don my hat and warm jacket. The recent frosts have broken up the soil nicely and in a few weeks' time I think I can most probably plant a few vegetables out. I find my tools in the lean-to and am so tempted to get up into the loft and find out what is going on up there. I move a few things to get to the rickety old wooden step ladder that leads up to the attic door, which is under the eaves. Very carefully I place a foot on the bottom rung, it creaks a little but takes my weight. I move on up and shudder as black sticky cobwebs stick to my hat, the door is small and has a large padlock on the bolt, I give it a bit of a jiggle the metal padlock is strong, luckily the wood is old and weak, one more yank and the bolt and padlock come away in my hand. I push the door and nothing happens, in true burglar style I need a crowbar to prise it open. I put the bolt and padlock in my pocket and ungainly climb down backwards, as I reach the bottom, I feel like a child caught out misbehaving as a voice says, 'Excuse me can I ask what you are doing? and why have you got a padlock sticking out of your pocket? I hope you have not vandalised the lock and attic door. As I have said before you only rent the croft and have no access to anywhere else.' Like a child I take the tell-tale items out of my pocket and hand them over. 'I need to talk to you about a few things,' I quietly say. 'Talk to my agent,' he sharply retorted. I was not going to let it go, I told him about the rats in the roof, he said it was quite impossible as there was no access for vermin to get in as the roof was made of stone. I assured him I was not lying and it was not fair to have to listen to that awful noise at night, as I had come all this way to get some peace and quiet and as yet I had experienced nothing, but weird happenings and then I felt tears well up and before I knew it, I lost my composure and fled indoors, before I embarrassed myself any further. Inside I didn't quite know what to do with myself, all I knew was that nothing felt right anymore, there was not one thing that hadn't changed in my life even my face in the mirror was quite different, the once happy face had been replaced by a serious expressionless one. I cannot think that I will ever feel anything other than this constant treadmill, barely bumbling through each day and nothing to look forward to anymore. I think I am tired of trying and hoping everything will feel better tomorrow, of course the changes in grief are slow and not always readily noticed. I know I will never get over it because you cannot erase all that love, but they will always be with me by my side.

I feel as if I am at a distance from reality and have been thrust into this strange world where I am alone trying to find a pathway. I know what I want, and that's to wake up from this nightmare and find none of the sadness in my head was real. But of course, that is quite impossible, sometimes I barely keep a grip on my sanity, in my head, I hear a scream that one day I fear will never stop. Even though time has made the gap bigger and bigger the scenario that rolls through my waking moments is as fresh as yesterday. Time, the great healer. how much time? I teeter on the edge of insanity.

When I think the coast is clear I leave the house, intending to spend the day outside, with the wildlife in hopes of grounding my irritability. The overcast sky fits my mood and I take the hill road inland. There is a slight touch of spring painting the winter landscape with a hue of fresh green life. The hawthorn trees are becoming alive again. In the distance I can see the hares racing each other in their spring cavort. There is just a slight sea breeze today and the sea is all the colours of the sky. The tide is far out and I stop to watch a dark shadow far out in the sea, at first, I think it must be a ship passing across the horizon and then more shadows appear and I realise I am watching a pod of whales, something I've heard so much about but never seen. I don't know how long I stood there, I watched until they finally sank into the depths of the ocean. The higher I walked the lighter my mood became, the further away from the croft the weight on my shoulders became lighter, I need time to think about the events that have happened since I moved here and if there is anything, I can do about them.

There aren't many trees here and the ones that have survived the strong winds show stunted growth and lean precariously inland, they give the appearance of scarecrows waving their wild twiggy arms. I take a path that is new to me and am surprised to see it leads inland, the view is beautiful and the fields roll away in front of me, a river meanders through the countryside and disappears between the rocks leading out towards the sea. A weak sun tries to push its way through the dense cloud, not enough to warm my face but so good to see. The grass is lush and green and the sheep busily graze, not taking any notice of me as I amble through their field. A few birds circle overhead and squeal as they dive and rise on the thermals. In front of me I can see a small bridge that crosses the river and I stop for a while to watch the stream, it is running so fast, the water is crystal clear and you can see the pebbles and stones at the bottom. Bright green reeds move quickly with the rush of the water, looking closer I can see black and green eels making their way up stream, before the tide turns and drags them back. I decide not to go much further and make my way back following the river, eventually I should come out at the sea not far from the bay. Along the way I see where there is evidence of otters, something I read about in the wildlife book. I would love to see them, but I think I am too noisy and impatient to wait quietly for them to appear. The muddy patch they have left behind has a collection of shell fragments and many tiny footprints. I move along the bank and notice a lot of the tufts of dead grasses and rushes beside the water have new green spikes poking through the golden dry mass. I look for other signs of life returning to the land and am pleased to see small gnarly bushes covered in small buds and think these must be the sweet Bilberry, in my mind, I make a mental note about Bilberry preserve, I'll have to check when the fruit will be ripe enough to harvest. I am amazed at how much edible food grows in the wild, so much healthier than buying a jar from the supermarket full of unknown chemicals and preservatives that we absorb when we eat them.

I am now walking towards the sea and I can feel the change in the breeze, I pull up my hood and find just one glove in my pocket, I need them on elastic like a small child. The sun has given up and is permanently hiding behind the evening cloud that is gathering on the horizon. I feel the chill as I walk around the headland, the tide is well on its way in and the water gently ripples onto the sand. Sea birds are oblivious of the water and busily forage on the shoreline, picking and poking, finding their supper, the only sound is the slight whistling of the wind and the occasional movement of the pebbles, being raked over by hungry beaks. This walk has had the desired effect on my jumbled mind, I could stay here with this feeling forever, I sit on a rock and trail my gloveless fingers through the brackish water in the rockpool, it is cold but soothing, I can feel the strands of seaweed and the soft edges of the rocks that are coated with green mossy vegetation. The sea edges nearer and the birds move back onto the shingle, quite oblivious of me, I wish I could bottle this moment and take a swig every now and again. Out here in nature everything that was unsettling my mind seems to be put into its perspective, even the hopeless grief that fills my every waking moment is tempered by nature. It is hard to describe the feeling of being so small in something so vast. A soothing hug engulfs me as Mother nature says, 'It is okay, I know why you are so sad, you have come so far, rest with me a while and let me comfort you and ease your pain.' I don't know how long I stayed, but I remember the sun setting and the chill that woke me. I made my way back to the croft and felt that something within me had definitely changed, not drastically but something was different.

The days that followed were taken up with daily walks around the island, wind or rain I made myself go out, often I would try and make an excuse, but then I would remember how exhilarating I would feel when I saw a new bird, lamb or a sprig of blossom, then my routine of walking became addictive and I could not stay indoors. I embraced all weathers and as the spring came and the mornings were lighter and warmer, I got out of bed a little earlier and walked further each day. I tended the small allotment in the garden in the afternoons and it started to resemble something other than a patch of mud. The apple trees in the orchard were fully dressed in pale pink blossom the best they had ever been according to Tom.

In a few days' time, Tom is bringing me a couple of pregnant sheep to keep in the orchard, apparently his boss had suggested it, at first, I was a little apprehensive as to why, but then the thought of lambs in the garden got the better of me, I have fenced off the veg patch and made the orchard secure. I still hadn't any bees in the hives and thought it was a shame, as they would have enjoyed the apple blossom. Builders are coming sometime to do a few repairs and I have quite a list for them. I did manage to talk to the agent about all the things that need doing, mainly the noises from the loft and now a wet patch has appeared above the kitchen and seems to be getting bigger, a few days after my phone call Tom came to check on all the repairs. I was so pleased because I expected a visit from surly Simon Blake and I was so ready for him, luckily for me he was away on one of his sabbaticals to Italy.

NOTHING IS PERMANENT.

Today I have actually left my polo neck off and opened the windows, the place is so different in the sunshine. I can see new birds arriving on the beach and there is a definite change in the countryside, the barren canvas of the winter has been painted by nature and it is such a miraculous change. I am so glad I came in the winter and have had the chance to see this all unfold by the day. The sun is such an amazing planet, it gives us light and warmth bringing life to the dormant earth. My walk today was to the other side of the island, I watched the comical puffins nesting in their burrows, they look as though they had been hand painted, what busy little birds they are, I had only ever seen them in books before I moved here. The dead trees of the winter have suddenly burst into life and are covered in bright green leaves shrouding the small patches of blue bells that hide beneath them, small flowers a native species not the big blousy ones that I am used to, they mix with wild anemones, perfect bedfellows.

On my windowsill I have a variety of young seedlings, in fact hundreds perhaps even thousands, it didn't look much when I opened the packets, just a sprinkle of dust but when I threw them into the seed tray, they waited a week then grew a forest of gangly plants, all I have to do now is to pluck up the courage to cruelly thin them out, what a decision to make, Tom said throw the weaklings away. Oh dear, I am so glad I made the decision to sow the broad bean seeds separately.

The wet patch on the ceiling seems to have grown since the last downpour and I will be pleased when the builders come, I am not looking forward to the disruption, on the other hand it will be good to get the jobs done. The front door is barely hanging on its hinges, Tom said they will repair the door as this one is the original and my landlord is into conservation and wants to preserve everything in keeping. Sounds like he's a bit stodgy and obsessive about the croft, it's a wonder he lets anyone live here. I am sure I have heard his car sometimes in the evenings, I think he comes to check on what changes I have made to his precious property. I would love to be able to have a normal conversation with him about his missing ancestor, I did sort of mention it to Betty and she was a little hesitant when I told her that I thought the girl who keeps hanging around the place is something to do with her boss. The annoying thing is, just when I think she has left, she pops up outside, and has taken to hanging around the orchard, her appearance has changed so much, each time I see her she looks thinner and unkept and now I am starting to believe she is not of this world but an unrested spirit. I have read about these people who cannot leave this world when they die and spend their time in limbo until they right some wrong doing. What am I saying, have I lost all sense of reason? what other explanation could there be for her to be here, Luca would say, 'Get a grip, you're losing it.' I think I lost it when he died, it certainly changes you and everything around you.

I can see a tractor and trailer coming down the road and hope Tom is bringing the ewes he promised me, the orchard is the perfect place for them and I'm sure the bees won't mind and of course the ghost.

Tom handles the sheep with an expert hand and after a lot of pushing, shoving and coaxing, they reluctantly stroll down the ramp onto the grass. He assures me they will be no trouble as they usually look after themselves, he said he would call back in a few days' time, to make sure I am happy with them.

I now have two beautiful woolly pregnant ewes in the orchard, such a perfect timeless scene, along with the apple blossom and beehives. At first these bundles of cream curls, remained in the same position Tom had left them in, and just when I thought they were not going to move from that spot, they turned on their heels and ran across the orchard and began mowing the grass. I can't wait for the lambs to be born, there is something about new born animals in the spring, up on the hills they are being born daily, each time I pass I see a few more newcomers. I can't help but notice how quickly the countryside is changing which is so good for me as I came here in the most, coldest darkest time of the year, it is such a different place when the sun shines.

The arrival of the bees is next on my list, I phoned Rob and he said the spring was a good time to set up a new hive. His friend Jake said it would be a good idea for me to hire the bees from a local club for a season and then he would collect them for the winter as they needed feeding throughout the cold months. I am so looking forward to their arrival, this is something that Luca and I were going to do together. I am very excited and apprehensive and have done a slight refresher course on the internet, Rob has assured me he is always at the end of a phone and would only be too pleased to help. The hives are against the stone wall and look a little bit too freshly painted and new, it will be nice when they blend in a little more with a coating of lichen with shrouds most objects here that don't move.

Just when things are going a little smoother there is always something waiting in the background wanting attention. The old washing machine in the scullery has developed a grating noise, it still seems to wash okay but the sound is becoming quite deafening and it has started to wander around the kitchen when it's trying to spin dry, I can't bear the thought of reporting yet another repair to the agent, I have already been reminded that this is a holiday let not a permanent residence. I should have mentioned it to Tom when he was here, he seems a lot more sociable than the agent in London or the right horrible Simon Blake.

As the day is so beautiful, I thought I would walk to the farm and talk to Tom, if I go across country it is not as far as driving and besides, I have all day. I leave a small window open in the croft to air the place, as the patch on the ceiling is getting worse, if they don't hurry up, I will get it done myself, it will be a lot quicker. Even though it's a beautiful day I put on my warm coat and stuff my gloves in the pocket as here the weather can change in a blink of the eye. Once away from the cottage I reluctantly turn on my mobile, it stays blank for a while and then as the precious signal beams across the sea it bursts into life, I thumb through all the e-mails and delete all the rubbish, a few are of interest, one about the plug plants I have ordered, another from Rob saying he will be bringing the bees on Friday, he's not sure what time as he's catching the ferry from the mainland. The last e-mail is from the agent for the estate saying that the builders have been delayed and no work can be undertaken on the roof before June. If the agent could have heard my reply, I am pretty sure he would have turned a beautiful shade of red. I suppose there is not a lot I can do about the delay, I reply to the e-mail informing the man that the washing machine is on the blink, he doesn't reply. Now I've reported it there is not much point going to see Tom. I continue my walk and decide to have a closer look at the old ruin on the hill. The walk is so refreshing as the wind has lost a lot of its power and is now a gentle offshore breeze. I notice so many minute wildflowers tucked under rocks and nestled cosily between the lush new hillside grass. It is such a shame that the beautiful white sheep have been numbered with bright blue paint, I know that they are to match the lambs with their mothers but bright blue paint staining the lamb's soft fleecy new coats seems like graffiti, surely there must be another way to mark them perhaps collars or plastic bands like new born babies.

The ruins and graves must be centuries old, it's quite amazing how they have survived so long. The yellow lichen has masked any inscriptions that remain. Even though the church has long ago lost its roof and its congregation, it still feels like a sacred place. I am standing in what would have been the alter end, just grass and a few bits of the debris from the derelict walls have replaced any relic of religion, even so I can still feel that I am in a place of worship, I wonder who the people were, that climbed the hill every Sunday to say their prayers and worship. I can't imagine how much life must have changed since then.

I am not sure how long I stayed in the ruin but even now in its sad state there is a great sense of comfort to be had. I am in no hurry to leave and sit down on a pile of rocks. This place overlooks the sea and the beach, beside me a small brown mouse move swiftly in and out of the tunnels of rock that I am resting on, quite oblivious of my presence, I stay completely still, savouring the peace, with only the sounds of the gulls high above my head. Far down on the beach I can see a horse and rider splashing along the sand I am so glad that I am up here and my landlord is so far away. I am so reluctant to move and lose the peaceful feeling, but as always, there is something that spoils it.

Below me on the path are a couple of ramblers, I have seen them before and even though they seem to be quite pleasant I would rather selfishly savour this moment a little longer. As there is nowhere to hide, I wait for them. They quickly appear and are surprised to see me sitting here. I greet them and hope they will be pleasant, but move on quickly. But no, they shuffle up on the rock beside me.

I listen to their chatter about the walk and what am I doing up here and before I had a chance to find an answer to their questions, they carried on talking, giving me a complete rundown of their personal information and then with great gusto the complete guide to walking on the island. They had been coming for years and then they remembered our last conversation when they asked if I was going to open the croft for refreshments. When I could get a word in, I reminded them that I was sure the landlord would not approve, as I had mentioned to them before, and then Mrs. Rambler or Maud as she told me to call her, said that the last time she saw Simon who was actually her nephew she had mentioned it to him and he did not seem to be bothered. I didn't show my surprise, and thought what a great opportunity to find out a little more about the Blake family. I told them about the book I had been reading about her ancestors and wondered did Alice Blake ever turn up. The next hour was taken up in the family history, I learnt so much. Apparently, Maud's grandmother talked about it often saying her Mother believed the wayward girl came to a sorry end because of her strange behaviour. Alice was quite a wild child for that time, she would often be out on the island not returning for days, the family got used to her disappearing, so it was no surprise that nobody noticed her missing for quite a long time. I was so tempted to tell them about the ghostly figure that I had seen. Something stopped me as in the light of day it all sounded so far-fetched. Very quickly they changed the subject and wanted some information about myself, of course they asked the one question I had not shared with anyone here, 'Are you here on your own? Are you married? What made you come here; I did ask my nephew but he all he said was you were renting the croft indefinitely.' I thought carefully and before the silence embarrassed me, I offered just enough to satisfy their curiosity. 'I am a widow.' I saw Maud's face and could tell she had more questions for me, instead she said I was too young to be widowed and her nephew was a widower also, without appearing to be rude, I quickly said it was so nice to meet them but I had to leave as I wanted to walk on the beach before sunset.

My head was full of jumbled thoughts about Alice and Luca, this is what happens when I resurrect those thoughts which are well buried most of the time. Each time I tell someone I am a widow the freshness of my grief comes to the forefront of my mind and slaps it straight into my brain and I have to believe the reality of it all over again.

As I approach the beach the sun which was shrouded by bruised cloud pierces through, casting heavenly rays of light onto the still water. I am alone on the sand and the only company I have are the birds that circle overhead and the few that are foraging amongst the wet shingle. I am unsettled and realise that whatever I tell myself, solitude is a strange thing, if I am truthful, I don't know what I want, this is the first time I've ever been in this situation. My mind keeps going back to the conversation with Maud, I wish I had thought to mention the locket after all it might belong to her family.

With the sun slowly setting I make my way back home. The windows of the croft reflect the dusky glow and the whitewalls are tinted a warm orange. I check on the sheep and make sure the gate to the

orchard is secure and as I walk back, I notice the
ladder to the loft has been moved and the door is
open. I wonder if the builders have called whilst I was
out, I suppose they might have left it open to let the
air in to try and dry it out before they repair it. I
cannot help myself and before my sensible head can
warn me of the perils, my feet are on the rung of the
ladder and I am up staring into the dark dusty loft. My
hands feel for something to hold onto and grip sticky
cobwebs. Slowly my eyes grow accustom to the dim
light and I can just make out mounds of chaos and
junk. I work my way along a narrow track through the
rubble. I stop and try to work out where the damp
patch is on the ceiling below, I can see a bare patch
where the builders have cleared it ready to make the
repairs. Far up in the high roof a little late sunshine
beams through the skylight, illuminating a spot far
under the eaves, dust particles dance on the rays,
curiously I climb over old crates, and boxes
disturbing great plumes of ancient dust, that tickles
my nose, the whole roof shudders as I sneeze loudly
and then just as I thought to retrace my footsteps
across this dusty place, something catches my eye, a
book is poking out from beneath a battered tin trunk. I
edge forward and bump my head on the rafters as I
reach down to pull the tatty object out, the outer cover
is torn and faded but what a surprise when I open it,
the writing is in pencil and is surprisingly clear, it is
some sort of journal or diary, there are lots of
sketches and a few delicate water colours, I recognise
some of the places and then I realise what I have in
my hand, I think it must be, Alice Blakes personal
journal and diary. I quickly put the delicate piece of
history in my pocket, I am so excited to find this and

cannot wait to read it, I wonder why it is here and not with her family, surely this is a precious piece of family history and then I wonder if they actually know about it.

I carefully retrace my footsteps across the loft and awkwardly turn around to go down the ladder, luckily unlike last time I trespassed up here, there is no-one waiting for me at the bottom. I pull the door closed and cannot wait to read my quarry. I am not surprised when I see the haggard figure standing at the far end of the orchard, soon she will be to thin and weak to stand, she raises her hand and beckons me, I decide it is too late in the evening to follow my imagination and I also know as soon as I get near her, she will fade away and leave me with the thought that my disturbed mind might be creating the vision of someone I had read about. I stand for a long time watching the figure drift back and forward across the grass, the sheep behave as if nothing is happening around them, she stops by the beehives, what a vision if it wasn't so far-fetched, the sight of her with the bright white Bee-hives would have made a beautiful picture. I force myself to turn away and when I look back, she has gone. Inside I turn on the coffee machine and sit and make myself write all that has happened today in my diary, lest I will forget all the important things, I also make notes of all the things I need to mention to Maud next time I see her. The book from the loft is so brittle bits of the paper disintegrate as I turn the pages, the sketches are quite childlike and naïve but beautiful in their simplicity, the colours are delicate and obviously she had a love of wildlife and words.

'Life is the perfect gift, use it wisely and savour the moment.'

Alice wrote many words of wisdom for someone so young. I turn a few more crispy pages and then remember there has been a change of plans, Rob and his friend are bringing the bees in the morning and I need to be up and about reasonably early. It will be nice to see him again. It has been a good day today and I hope this is my turning point and I am so pleased to have discovered the journal and look forward to reading more.

The night was spent tossing and turning, the pillow seemed full of rocks and somehow the duvet turned sideways in the night and in my dreams my legs had grown too long. I was relieved when the sun rose and shone in my eyes, wearily I got out of bed and put my freezing feet on the icy cold floor. The sun was warm but weak and had no effect on the temperature in the room. Steam spiralled up as the kettle boiled, I relished the heat from it. Pulling on my dressing gown I looked at my seeds growing on the window sill, some have grown so much I will need to pot them on before they get root bound, so many jobs to do, how did I ever find time to go to work. I wash and dress quickly, putting on my gardening clothes ready for Rob to arrive. I look forward to him visiting he is such a happy person and really chatty. The wind has dropped today and the temperature is rapidly rising, the spring can be roasting hot or frosty cold, I don't think the earth can make up its mind when the seasons change. According to my diary it is Easter next weekend, not that it will make any difference to me at all except there will be more ramblers and visitors to this part of the island, I don't blame them because each day the wildflowers and wildlife become more radiant after the long bleak winter it's absolutely an amazing change to the countryside.

Rob and his bee keeper friend Jake were really late bringing the bees; they were buzzing and humming furiously in their box, Jake explained to me about settling the bees in their new hives, I told him I had been on a course, but he ignored me and carried on with many do's and don'ts. I was really eager to get them into their new home. The orchard was looking the best it could possibly be, the apple trees were dripping with bunches of fragrant blossom, nestled underneath was a blanket of bluebells with a scattering of celandines making a perfect spring carpet. Jake sealed the hives and gave me yet more instructions he seemed reluctant to leave me alone with the precious bees. To break the intensity of the situation I suggested coffee and flapjacks, Rob got the gist of my diversion and guided Jake into the front garden where I had put out a couple of chairs and a rickety table I had found under the lean-to. Jake was restless and jittery, he insisted on checking on the hives, it gave Rob a chance to ask me if I would like to go with him to a Ceilidh on the island on Sunday evening, he played a fiddle in a band and he thought it would be a good way of me to meet some of the locals, he said I had hidden up here long enough and it wasn't good for anyone to be alone for so long. I wanted to refuse his offer as it sounded dreadful, not me at all and then he said he would pick me up at seven thirty and I had nothing to worry about as I would be safe with him and it wasn't far. I will never know what made me agree to his invite, when he and Jake left, I instantly regretted the decision I had made.

I was annoyed I had given myself another thing to worry about.

No sooner had Rob left than the landlords Range Rover appeared outside, complete with a trailer containing a washing machine, it looked older than the broken one. Just what I needed a grumpy man in my kitchen. I gathered up the empty cups and plates and took them into the indoors. Of course, the man never missed anything and immediately assumed I was selling teas and cakes from the croft. I let him ramble on about his aunt mentioning me doing refreshments and before he could tell me off, I told him I made coffee for friends and there was nothing in my lease about that or was he going to add that as another stupid rule. He went quite red faced and stopped talking. I left him to disconnect the old washing machine and struggle in with the new one. I watched him heave the machine into the small space and kindly offered a plaster when he scraped his knuckles on the draining board. I tried to get on with tidying all the bits of paper that had accumulated on the small table. The atmosphere felt really awkward and just as I thought to offer him a coffee, he switched the machine on and the noise blocked out any conversation. I put the coffee machine on and signalled to him pointing to a cup. He nodded, I brushed past him and washed out the mugs I had used for Rob. Beside him I felt extremely small as he was towering above me like a giant, it's a shame I feel so intimidated by him. He told me the machine seemed to be okay and I handed him the coffee and just when I thought this moment is okay, he said, 'Try not to overload it, that's the quickest way to wear out the bearings.' I retorted instantly, that I am one person, how much washing do you think I get.' I felt my eyes blazing and again I was on the defensive. 'No that is not what I meant, why do you turn everything around, it's a fact that too much heavy washing wears the machine out quicker than if you split the load.' I looked at him with the contempt he deserved and shook my head in despair. 'Do you have a problem with me, because you cannot help but be rude and arrogant and I can honestly say I don't know why.' I left that thought with him whilst I went to look at the hives. He followed me out into the orchard, I listened to the buzzing coming from the hives, they were all sealed in till they settled. 'I think you should move the hives away from there and put them in under the trees, it looks quite dark and damp where they are in the shadow of the wall, you must realise you have to keep them happy.' I asked if he actually knew anything about bees and he assured me he was quite an expert and had many hives at the farm and the honey in the farm shop was from his bees, also the pure wax candles and polish were made from them. This was the most I had ever heard him speak without telling me off. I admitted I did wonder about the hives so near to the wall and Rob had also initially mentioned it. He said he thought that it was Rob and Jake he passed on the way here. Rob and him apparently were at school together on the island. He offered to move the hives and I thanked him and went to refill the coffee mugs. He stayed for a while wandering around the orchard looking at the trees, he mentioned they were really old and that his grandfather had planted them when he renovated the croft after it had been left empty for a long time. I plucked up courage and asked about his ancestor

Alice who had disappeared, he said that Betty had mentioned that I had seen a girl in the garden and whereabouts and I'd thought that she was a ghost, and he asked what had happened to make me think that. I was a little taken back by his question. In the grim light of day, I felt foolish talking about my thoughts on the ghost girl, he made it all sound so stupid. I stuttered and stumbled over my reply and felt really uncomfortable. He listened and then said he didn't believe in that sort of thing and added when your dead your dead. Then he added that when some people lose someone close to them, they get comfort from believing their loved one was still alive, living in another dimension as a spirit. I couldn't reply and suddenly thought to myself what the hell am I doing talking to this man, all I wanted to do was get away from him, this conversation is not what I wanted to hear especially from a man I disliked immensely. I made some feeble excuse and hurried indoors and closed the door. I was not sure what I was feeling, angry, stupid, sad and really weary. He had made me realise the reality of death and grief and I hated him for it. He knocked the door before coming in and I turned away from him as I didn't want him to have the pleasure of seeing the effect his frankness had on me. He walked to the sink and I heard his keys jangle as he retrieved them. He mumbled something that sounded like an apology and closed the door. I now know the expression, 'Taking the wind, out of your sails.' Again, I feel absolutely deflated and realise all this, moving here and trying to forge a new life far away from the tragedy is just a way of hiding from anything that could possibly remind me of the sad, sudden loss of the two people that formed my family.

Grief never leaves you it follows you wherever you go, at first like a lead overcoat and then the coat gets a little lighter and then it becomes a second skin slightly uncomfortable but part of you.

I leave the croft and walk, not stopping, this is the only way I know how to ease the creeping thoughts that want to take me back to that time that changed my life to this lonely existence that no-one can change, its real, not a nightmare to wake up from or someone else's sad story. I am oblivious of anything around me and feel the cool spring rain on my face, hoping it will wash away all the fears and tears that seem to have plagued me for the last two years. I reach the top of the hill and stand, savouring the silence, I turn to face the sea and all I see is a vast turquoise green expanse disappearing far into the horizon and I am instantly jealous of a beautiful large noisy white Herring gull that is soaring high above the cliffs, diving down to glide just above the water, I am free as that bird but envy his simple life, I carry too many thoughts, my mind is constantly overthinking, so many, if's and and's. Well, I realise I can't be a bird, this is it I am Alice with all the baggage in my mind that I seem to collect on a daily basis, I turn and my legs carry on walking, I don't know where I am going but my feet won't stop, I pass the sheep with their lambs and sadness fills me to their fate, my mood stays in the doldrums and my crazy imagination is quite out of control thinking of all the depressing things that could only make me feel worse. It is not long before I feel a presence walking along beside me, I don't need to look, my skin creeps as Alice Blake is so close to me, I can feel her anguish, I am frightened to look and keep my eyes straight ahead, I can see from the corner of my eye the fragments of her dress touching my arm. I wonder if she only appears when I am sad and perhaps Simon is right, I am imagining her as I want to believe you never die. Imagination or not she is so close beside me I can hear her sobbing; I cannot help but look at her and I recoil as this poor girl is so emancipated and yet I can see through the stretched skin a young desperate girl. Her slender fingers grip my arm and I stop walking. I reach out to touch her and she is real flesh and blood, I ask her how can I help, she moves away from me and walks back down the path towards the croft. I follow, her dress is now torn into shreds and soiled, you can only just make out the embroidered pattern on it, she is so very slight the fine fabric falls off her thin frame, her blonde hair is matted and clumps have fallen out leaving her scalp exposed. For a moment I have the feeling of losing my sanity and the thought exhausts me, I aimlessly follow the girl, we arrive at my gate and I expect her to go into the cottage but she goes straight through the fence and into the orchard, at that moment I finally realise she is not of this dimension and even though I can see her and feel her touch she is definitely not human anymore. She stands in the shadows by the wall, I stay by the front of the house and watch her, her bony fingers drag out strands of her hair, they slowly float down to nestle amidst the spring flowers, her mouth opens and she silently screams, the vision is horrifying, I can't watch her anymore, this is becoming part of my living nightmare. I turn away from the spectacle and when I look back, she has gone and the sheep have moved to where she stood, I carefully pick up the locks of her hair that lay gently amongst the bluebells, indoors I tuck the tresses between the crumpled pages of her journal, I am now totally convinced she is Alice Blake and she wants me to find her body, I need to make a note of all the sightings of her and the events in my diary before I forget them or become too insane to recall them. I throw a baking potato into the oven and settle down into my favourite chair, I write continually and work on this madness well into the evening only stopping occasionally to remember dates and times, it does not make sane reading, what in heavens name is happening to me I must get a grip on myself; I have become so much more troubled since I came here.

Eventually exhausted I finish writing, I stay sitting in the window and watch the clouds move slowly across the tranquil sea and try to quieten my mind, I know deep down I am going to have to make a lot of decisions for my future, this is no way to live, I need to take a serious look at the strange life I seem to have created here, I have made the pain of grief so much worse by running away from it, I have lost the comfort of familiar surroundings and all the things that stood for my life, I have no stable home, only chaos. But first I owe it to Alice to find out more about her, she has chosen me for some reason and it doesn't matter what people think or believe I will not let her down.

THE NURTURED SEED GROWS IN ALL IT'S GLORY.

I have worked endlessly in the garden today and all my plants are interred in the vegetable patch and I have taken the covers off the bees so at last, they are free, straight away they busily gorged on the apple blossom, I have constructed a sort of haphazard cold frame and filled it with tomato, cucumber and melon plants. I envisage all the wonderful fruit veg and honey that will be produced by the end of the season.

Rob messaged me this morning to say that he hoped I had not forgotten that he was picking me up tonight, I wasn't quick enough to think of a feasible excuse. I have showered in freezing cold water as the gas bottle has run out again, I am reluctant to phone Tom for a refill in case he sends his employer with it. I throw on a white blouse and clean jeans and find my Aran sweater, even though we are well into spring the evenings can still be chilly. I hear Rob's van long before it appears in the lane. As I lock the front door, he turns the van around, as I climb into the passenger seat, I catch a glimpse of something out of the corner of my eye, I look back as we leave, Alice stands forlornly watching us leave, her skeletal face is so disturbing. Rob asks if I am alright as I look like I have seen a ghost, I give a slight laugh and say, 'If only you knew.' He smells manly, of soap and linseed oil and is dressed in a check shirt and is also wearing an Aran jumper. I am a little surprised when just after a few miles he turns into Weathercote farms drive. I comment on this and he said he thought he had told me the dance was in the barn on the farm and he added that Simon always let them use it for their get togethers. He assured me it would be really bustling and good fun. I knew I should have refused his offer and wondered how long it would take me to walk back home. He parked in the courtyard and there seemed to be lots of other cars there. The barn was enormous and smelt of straw, at one end was a table with a variety of alcohol and soft drinks on and at the opposite end was a wooden stage made out of pallets, decked with an assortment of amplifiers and musical instruments, straw bales were arranged around the floor for seating. Rob introduced me to a few people and the left me with a juice sitting on a hay bale near the stage whilst the band tuned their instruments, I could not have felt more out of place if I had tried. The barn started to fill up and I can honestly say I recognised no-one and then the lovely Jake the bee-keeper, loomed up in my face and I knew the evening was going to be a long one. I was so pleased when the music started and it was so loud that it drowned out the monotonous drone of the lecture, I was getting on bee keeping.

The music was lively and a few people danced I declined the offer from Jake and said I enjoyed just watching, he wandered off and persuaded an older lady to the floor. I tried not to look at my watch, I was suddenly so relieved to see Tom and Betty enter the barn, Betty carried a large plate of her delicious scones and as she put them on the table, she saw me and smiled, soon she was sitting beside me saying how good it was to see me enjoying myself and she was so sorry that I was a widow at such a young age and it must have been really difficult to travel all the way from London to live here on my own. I thought how news travels fast on a small island, again the music drowned out all the questions she wanted to ask about my personal life, but I knew it would only be a matter of time. Maud must have been really busy with her news I suppose it's out now, 'London, orphan and widow, leaves bright lights behind to become a hermit on a remote island.' I can't avoid the truth forever, I just don't want strangers discussing my loss, they didn't know them or me how can they begin to feel or understand. It's my grief, my nightmare and no-one will be-little it with empty condolences, sometimes you don't want advice, just someone to listen.

The music suddenly ended, and swiftly merged into another tune, a monotonous dirge with what felt like a hundred sorrowful verses, that all sounded the same as the one before, luckily it was still too noisy for conversation, I could feel Betty's hopeful anticipation of a break in the music and a chance for me to fill in her questionnaire, the sad song finally ended and after a round of applause the band retired to the bar for a break. For some reason I expected Rob to notice me or at least look my way, but he seemed to be deep in conversation with the other band members discussing what music to play for the next half of the night. Never in my wildest dreams would I have ever imagined myself at one of these back of beyond shindigs, I've been to festivals in Hyde Park and summers at Glastonbury and sat through live performances at the 02, and because of the death of my husband I am here punishing myself with bad music and I hear my inner self remind me, 'It's your choice, no-one made you.'

I ask Betty where the loo is and she says we are to use the one in the back porch of the house and she offers to show me. We walk out of the bright lights into the darkness and for just a moment I am totally blind, I stumble and trip over the uneven cobble stones of the courtyard and fall forward, my hands reach out blindly in front of me, my knees hit the ground before the rest of my body, I feel really stupid and quickly right myself. Betty starts to fuss and wants to take me into the house and look at my knees, I decline her offer and tell her I am fine, in the toilet I can see I have got the knees of a seven-year-old in the school playground all scrazed and bloodied, my jeans have saved me from further injury. I confidently tell Betty I am really okay and I am going home, she looks concerned and I assure her I know a short cut across the fields and I will soon be there. I am so relieved to leave the barn and make a note to say, 'NO,' next time, if ever there is one. My knees smart as I bend my legs to climb over the stile, from here I can see the last rays of the sun setting over the water and the colours are of spun gold playing on the slow receding ocean. I walk diagonally across the vast field, I can see a few sheep grazing, they lazily glance at me and quickly resume their munching, I pull my sweater around me as the wind whips around the headland and instantly changes the temperature, I am not sure exactly how far I have to walk, but I would rather endure a marathon than another moment in the barn, feeling so awkward in such unfamiliar surroundings. My feet seem to be walking automatically unaware of my sore knees.

After what seemed like an hour trudging on my stiff legs, I feel so relieved when I can see the faint outline of the croft nestled far down in the valley. My bloody knees are drying and sticking to me jeans and as I climb over another stile, I wince quite loudly and then without any reason, it occurs to me how alone I really am, at this moment, there is absolutely no-one to hear me or comfort me, no-one for me to tell about all the things that have happened and no-one to put strong arms around me and make me feel safe. Even in the barn crammed with happy people I felt alone, I was the stranger, consumed by sadness and almost resenting the way everyone was blissfully unaware of my private thoughts and enjoying themselves.

My selfish thoughts take me across another vast green space and in the gloom, I can see yet another stile, I haul myself over the steep wooden step and am thankful to find myself in familiar surroundings. I am half way down the stony path that leads up to the ruins any other time I would be eager to sit on the stones and watch the night sky drift in over the sea, but tonight I just want to get indoors and tend my wounds. As I walk down the lane my phone hums in my pocket, the signal is quite good up here and I see that Rob is calling me, he asks where I am and what happened, I briefly tell him, he laughs and says he'll catch up with me next time, I thank him for taking me and pluck up courage and tell him it's not really my thing and if he doesn't mind, I'll give it a miss. 'Your loss,' he says and abruptly rings off.

Just a short downhill trek and I am reaching in my pocket for my key, the croft feels like a sanctuary and I sink into a chair. I sit for a while and reflect the evening; I am glad in a way I tried to go out and feel I have offended Rob, one of the only friends I've got here. I make a note to call him tomorrow and apologies for my rudeness, after all his music is his passion and I think I most probably insulted him about the evening. I seem to have forgotten how to behave in company something else I will blame my grief state for, I have lost my moral compass and need to find the real me, the one who is not so angry all the time, the me who thinks before she speaks and the me who is kind, perhaps she has gone and this is the new me, I wish time would pass quicker as everyone tells me it takes time to get over a loss but, no-one tells me how long and what will I be like at the end of this expected time. will I be back to my normal self whoever that is or will I be an aggressive, miserable old lady resenting happy youths, this no-one can tell me.

I sit on the edge of the bath and peel my jeans off my sore knees, I am shocked at the amount of blood for something so small. My knees look bruised and are not attractive at all, very soon I cover my wounds with plasters, thank goodness I brought a first aid box with me. The aroma of antiseptic mixes with the mustiness of the cottage and omits a strange smell. I open a fanlight window and hope the night air will dilute the toxic fumes.

I am snuggled into my soft fleecy blanket with a hot chocolate and about to read Alice Blakes journal when the room is lit up by headlights coming down the hill, I expect it to be Rob coming to see if I am alright, I pull my dressing gown around me and hobble to the door. The bright lights dazzle me and I shield my eyes, a figure walks towards me and I am surprised to see Simon standing in the shadows. Somehow, I feel awkward and hesitate to ask him to come in. He says that Betty told him about my fall and as he's legally libel for anyone who has an accident on his land, he thought he should come and see if I was alright, and before I could answer he asks if I had consumed a lot of alcohol. My hackles went up in seconds and I quickly retorted that he should not worry I was not in the habit of drinking alcohol and perhaps he should sort out his cobbles if he was going to invite the public there. He appeared more worried about his own skin than my damaged knees and then to top it all he asked if I was wearing suitable shoes or high heels. In sheer disbelief I looked him straight in the eye and slowly closed the door. I was too tired to be bothered with this pathetic man.

I tried not to let his visit upset me, but the conversation kept going through my head, Luca used to say to me when I over stressed about things was, 'Only worry about things you can do something about. If you can't then don't waste your energy.' It's a true piece of advice. I think about the conversation and realise I can only account for my thoughts and not Simon's, he will think what he will and I am not willing to waste my time trying to change his arrogant mind. My knees throb and I stretch my legs out to ease them. Alice's journal seems to be deteriorating a bit like she is and the aged paper is becoming quite dry and crisp. I gently flick through the pages of illustrations with comments written in pencil and find it all changes and there are hastily written notes faded with time but still readable. And then it all takes a sudden change in tone and I am wide awake.

I can't believe what has happened to me. If only Laddie had not barked and snarled at the men, they would never have seen me, When I saw them coming, I was quick and I hid behind all the boxes, but Laddie didn't like the men and he made such a noise and they found me. they were so angry when they saw me amongst the flagons and tea chests. I know my father has been looking for these men who smuggle goods to save paying taxes, he will be so pleased when I tell him who they are.

I am so glad they didn't find my book and pencil; they were in my pocket deep inside my cloak. I wish that they had not taken my bag with all my paints in and my lunch, and what will they do with Laddie. I heard him bark in the night, but he is silent now, if he runs back home, they will wonder where I am and come and find me.

Why have they put me up here, what have I done. I promised I wouldn't tell anyone about all the boxes, but they were horrible to me and would not listen, now I will tell.

I think I have been here for one night and a day. The roof is leaking and I am getting wet.

I am getting quite hungry.

When my father finds me, he will have them all hanged.

I recognised two of the men, George our stable boy and his father whom I have never liked, as he could be quite cruel to the horses. George whispered to me that he would bring me some food and water and not to make a noise as it would upset his father.

Another night has passed and I can see the stars high up through the skylight, they chained me to the roof beams and I cannot move very far, I have called and shouted but I think no-one except the men will ever come to this place, only they know I am here and I fear they will not come back to release me.

I thought in my dreams I heard Laddie barking far away down on the beach.

I think today I could hear people talking downstairs, I shouted and called but I think they ignored my calls.

I feel so hungry today and even though it is raining and the roof is leaking I cannot reach the drip that is making a wet pattern on the floor. I feel really uncomfortable and my clothes are getting quite damp and dirty. When I get home, I am going to have a lovely warm bath and I hope cook will bake me some warm scones and I will fill them with sweet jam and cream fresh from the cows.

I am sure Father must be missing me, why hasn't he come to find me. I heard horse riders outside the croft a few days ago but the wind was blowing and so noisy I don't think they could hear me. I screamed and shouted till my throat was so sore and my voice was just a whisper.

I don't know the names of the other men that captured me and put me up here but I suspect they are the smugglers that my Father talks about, I have watched them often in the caves and on the shoreline and I have sketched them often.

I feel so tired and my stomach is rumbling and aching.

A large bird flew over the skylight today and I wished he could see me and tell someone.

I dreamt of my bedroom and my mother; she will be so worried.

My pencil is getting blunt and the sharpener was in my bag. I have been here four days and I have still not eaten. I have never worn such soiled clothes. I think Father will find me today.

I cried a lot today, I miss my family so much, how can they not come. I am cold and my eyes are misty, I think my salty tears made my eyes dry. I don't want to die up here on my own, I am frightened and don't know what to do. I am going to scream some more. Help. Help me please.

I have tried praying over and over again, but I fear God is cross with me and is punishing me for all the times I have misbehaved, I swear I will never be bad again.

Last night was really cold, I managed to drag an old carpet from under the eaves and wrap myself in it, it was so dusty it made me cough and sneeze and now it is heavy and wet.

My throat is really sore and I can hardly swallow. I just want to lie down; I am so cold.

I really don't want to write today.

George has not brought me food. Please God help me.

I dreamt I was at home in my warm bed with mother sitting in her chair reading to me and then I woke up and realised, I think I am dying.

My ankles are sore and swollen they're really painful.

I think I saw one of the men today, he stood over me, I tried to talk but my throat was too painful I reached out to him, he stepped back and said to someone, 'She's still alive.' I silently pleaded for help but he disappeared through the trap door.

I am going to hide my journal under the eaves, because if the man comes back, I don't want him to see the picture I've drawn of him and his friends.

They came again and stood over me, someone gave me a drink. It was so bitter; I was so thirsty.

I can't breathe. I can't see to write anymore.

Mother and Father, I love you, please find me……

I cry for this poor girl and all she went through, just a few feet above my head in the dark loft, and I cry for myself and for Luca dying so young, I cry for losing my Mother in her prime of life, I miss and need them both so much, I am bumbling through some sort of life in a different dimension, getting up and going to bed the only sure things I can rely on, everything else is odd and feels strange.

My dreams are filled with the cries of a young girl calling for her mother, I keep waking up with a searing pain in my sore knees. Finally, I can't stay in bed any longer and decide to accompany the sunrise, the clock says four thirty-seven, so blessed early and yet so still and beautiful. I don my warm clothes and hobble outside to share the awakening of the countryside. The dawn chorus is slightly different here than in London, here the birds are mainly coastal and have an almost ghostly song, distant and echoing on the wind.

The apple trees are in full bloom, heavy with pink and white blossom, the constantly busy bees have started early, they are diving into the delicate flowers and shaking the petals loose, which drop to the ground like silent snowflakes. The sheep are still grazing and I am overjoyed to see that one has given birth to twins in the night, quite silently, mother and lambs are oblivious of me watching them. I remind myself to text Tom to let him know about the lambs. I lift the lid on the cold frame and am delighted to see strong runner bean shoots appearing from the pots and the peas have managed to creep up their sticks. Even with the sheep chomping there is a stillness to the morning. I stand and look at the ladder at the back of the woodstore, if my knees weren't so sore, I would have been tempted to rummage through the loft, but decide to leave it until my knees are a bit more mobile.

I am restless and feel compelled to visit the beach, the morning is so beautiful and there is something quite soothing and calming about the motion of the sea, the vastness and the pure strength of the waves, I was always told as a child to treat the ocean with great respect and never underestimate its unpredictability.

I am so disturbed by my sad discovery in the loft that my mind keeps going back to Alice, and however much I try to replace the thoughts with others she is embedded in my brain and I know until I solve this problem, I will have no peace.

I walk along the beach close to the fast-ebbing tideline and it is of no surprise to me to see the ghostly figure of Alice high up on the rocks looking far out to sea. I am instantly aware of her decrepit state, it is hard to look at her without wanting to run away as far as I could possibly go. She turns towards me and silently glides down the shingle path, as she nears, I hold my breath in repulsion, her shrunken body hardly fills the tattered dress that hangs from her skeletal frame. Alice's bony fingers reach out to me and I recoil in horror as I can actually feel the ghostly touch of her freezing cold flesh, I don't know how long she held my hand but an amazing thing happened, I can't believe my eyes and I suddenly can see her in a different light, she is not a walking corpse anymore but a fine young girl full of life, robust and brimming with good health. She holds my hand as we walk along the beach and I feel I know her really well, on her white slim fingers she wears a purple and green ring, that sparkles in the light. In front of us a collie dog has appeared from the caves and races towards us, as I reach down to stroke the dog Alice lets go of my hand and as I look up, I realise I am completely on my own even the dog has disappeared. I try really hard to understand what is happening to me.

Confused I turn to walk back to the croft. The birds are descending on the shoreline raking over the wet sand eating anything living that the tide has left behind, all so normal. I reach the croft, looking up on the rocks just in case she is there. Nothing, just the most amazing sunrise over the sea.

I have made my mind up that I have to go up into the loft and have a good look for any evidence of Alice, after all I did find her journal. Perhaps she was rescued and the journal means nothing and is not real at all, just her ramblings and yet my instinct tells me she tragically died in the attic and her restless spirit haunts the croft, and me. I think somehow because I was in a vulnerable state of grief, I was more susceptible, I wonder who I can trust with this new information, perhaps Maud after all she is a relation, of Alice's, definitely not Simon he would just give me another star on the, 'This woman is completely mad list.'

I did not enjoy my breakfast and throw the half-eaten toast out to the hungry Ravens that perch on my roof and make a hell of a din, a bird I have never seen flying free, only in the grounds of the Tower of London, or in wildlife parks in small cages. These scruffy black birds fly like witches and have an amazing wingspan. Some believe these black birds are messengers from the gods and carry a prophecy, I think they are just big black noisy birds that wait for my breakfast.

Tom has come to check out the lambs and painted bright blue numbers on them, such a shame. He asked me how my knees are and said his boss was concerned about the state of the courtyard and has arranged for the builders to make the cobbles safer. I kept my views to myself and changed the subject to the bees. He checked them over and said they seemed okay and then he surveyed my veg patch, occasionally raising his eyebrows and shaking his head. He gave me some useful advice on earthing up the potatoes and keeping the greenfly off the broad beans, I told him I am not using any chemicals on the garden and I was trying to grow everything organically, he wandered back to his car laughing his head off, his last words were as he drove away was something about, green gardeners and feeding the slugs.

My knees are throbbing as I get down on my haunches to plant a few rows of peas, I am sure the Ravens are just waiting for me to go indoors before they rob me of these little green gems. I walk around to the back of the house and find some long twigs that I can use as a bit of protection for the peas, there is plenty of debris on the ground after the winter winds, I collect an armful and am on my way back when I see Maud and her husband approaching the gate, what a coincidence, I am quite pleased to see her and invite them in. After what seemed like an hour of listening to her endless mindless boring chatter, I try and steer the conversation to her ancestor Alice Blake's disappearance. I tell her what I have found, but am reluctant to show it to her, not that she was at all interested in my conversation. She interrupted me a dozen times with some unrelated anecdote or another. I am so eager to tell her my theory about her ancestor, she is not at all interested and wants to tell me all about the size of her house and how she inherited it from her father and how her dear husband who was silently sitting beside her, was completely broke when she met him, and then without drawing breath or a comma she completely switched the conversation to ask about me, she suddenly apologised for me being a widow and asked what exactly had happened to my husband. She sat greedy eyed anticipating my reply, I said it had been a tragic accident, I hoped that would be enough to satisfy her, but I could see she needed more, wearily I knew this was the moment that I had managed to avoid so far since I had arrived on this island, the moment when I was going to delve into the hidden box that I kept securely close to my heart and give her the private personal information that left me broken. Defeated I briefly told her that he was in a car accident with my mother and they had both been killed. I hoped this information would have been enough, but as always people want all the gritty details. I sagged slightly and got up from my chair and with all my might I changed the subject to Alice again. I showed her the journal. She flicked through it, I could see she had no interest in it whatsoever, I went to the drawer and got out the locket, she said she doubted after all this time it couldn't possibly belong to the girl as she had never lived in the croft, I showed her the scribble in the book, she assured me it could never have survived this long and then I made the biggest mistake, I told her about the girl, the ghost, and then I saw her expression change and I knew I had gone too far. Very quickly she ushered her sad little husband out of the door, he turned to smile at me as she made excuses of having lunch with her nephew and didn't want to keep him waiting as he was such a busy man.

There are moments when I feel numb and distant to everything, and think I must have died in my old life and this is limbo, a place where I am a stranger and everything around me is uncomfortable, and I can't give up searching for the past life that I seem to have stepped out of. It is so hard to forge ahead trying to make a new normal, but I now know soon I will get used to this and even though I will never forget my soul mate and the man who held my heart and broke it, and who was the ultimate reason for my being, I will live alongside my grief, I have survived this long, my strength is returning and I can see a small glow at the end of the long tunnel. Each new day is a step further away from that tragic day and soon time will widen the gap and soothe the incredible feeling of not loneliness, but aloneness.

SEE CLEARLY THE WORLD IS FULL OF MIRACLES.

Each day I am making new discoveries, today I noticed for the first time, that, the oyster catchers all wear red stockings to   match their beaks, they have black and white hand painted intricate plumage, how can nature be so perfect. I have actually found my art materials and have made a naïve effort at starting a painting diary of the wild life that I come across on my rambles. I love the hills and moorlands but am drawn to the beach, if I don't manage to wander down to it to it each day then, I have withdrawal symptoms. There is a magic healing to the sounds of the tide gently moving the shingle and even when the wind blows and wild sea threatens to move the grey rocks that scatter the beach, it is invigorating and mood changing.

I have not seen Alice since I saw her as a normal healthy girl. Perhaps since I read her diary, she realised someone knew what had happened and is now at peace, or I am coming out of the shroud of trauma and my mind is repairing.

Luckily, I have been left alone since Maud's visit and have been quite happy in my solitude, even though Rob has been texting me about taking me to another dance in the barn. I reminded him about the last time and said I would rather spend my time here with my sheep, he obviously thought I was joking and said it was a spring solstice ceilidh and I couldn't possibly miss it. I must be a really weak person, so he is picking me up, I reminded him about my knees and he thought it was so funny. Secretly I am a little more eager than last time and I always know the scenic route home if I get bored.

Last night I was so restless and I am really pleased that I felt that way because, today I feel truly blessed. I had cooked the most amazing fresh fish, caught that morning and the croft wreaked, it carried the reminder of the meal well into the evening, I opened the windows that weren't jammed and ended up propping the front door open, had I not done that then I might have missed the most amazing spectacle. Over the sea the normal remnants of the sunset, had changed and the heavens were moving, swirling angels of misty blue danced across the night sky and as I wandered down to the beach a kaleidoscope of colours filled the horizon, great swathes of luminous green silently danced in the heavens, I have never ever observed such a spectacular event, ever changing colours and patterns, I don't know how long I stood there but I felt so at one with the universe and something changed within me, for the better, it was an awakening and an immense feeling of comfort, great warm arms held me and just for a moment I knew that Luca was near and I was not alone and it was okay, I know we will meet again but not just yet. The miracle in the sky was unexplainable and I realise there is so much more to this amazing world than I will ever know.

This morning the sunrise was quite amazing and I found myself out in the vegetable patch quite early. Even though the temperature is still low and the wind is relentless the seeds I put in are starting to grow, some of them are a little slow and windswept, the runner bean trench I dug when the weather was so wet is nearly filled with veg peelings and horse manure, I think today I am going to put up the sticks ready for planting them out at the end of the month, they are becoming quite unruly in the cold-frame and starting to wind themselves around the cauliflower plants.

The wind has dried out the earth nicely and today I think it will be quite easy to plant the onions and kale. The garden is not so messy as it was and I think I have made great use of it. I have found some old wooden planks and I think I can make some veg and herb boxes on legs so the slugs can't reach them, I should really ask Simon or Tom if I can use the wood but I really want to get on with my project without having to submit myself to a sharp refusal.

The bees seem to be settling down even though they appear to spend a lot of their time away from the garden up on the hills gorging on the spring flowers, I have planted so much lavender and hope eventually to supply them with all the flowers they need. I am so happy with these busy creatures I could watch them for hours; Luca would have loved them and I get comfort from doing something we both meant to do and of course I look forward to them producing aromatic honey. The village shop sells small glass jars with red checked metal lids which will be ideal for the honey, all I'll have to do is make my own labels.

I have so many seed packets and not really enough room for everything I want to grow so I think I will grow just a few of everything, Tom said it was best to stagger the planting so when I harvested one lot, another was on the way. I am keeping a log of what I've planted because I am starting to lose track, already I have lost some of the name tags I put at the end of the rows, so I will have to guess what they are when they start to grow. I have planted half a row of beetroot and the other half carrots and the next row a mixture of spinach and kale. Lettuces are now sown in a couple of enamel basins I found in the lean-to and I've nestled them on top of the stone wall in hopes the slugs don't like heights, I have also planted nasturtiums in between the large cracks in the wall, they should be vibrant and also attract the wild bees.

I have had an amazing morning, gardening is so good for a restless soul, especially when you see a small fine seed get warmth, light and water and suddenly swell and grow into a magnificent plant, such a miracle, all that just growing from a small speck of dust. Whilst I have been lost in my gardening world, I hadn't noticed my landlord was standing in the lane outside the croft looking at the roof. I thought to ignore him and kept my head down, pulling at a few imaginary weeds hoping he would do what he had to do and go away. Unfortunately, that did not happen. My heart sunk when he came in the gate and into my head, I was saying an affirmation over and over again, 'Please don't spoil my day, please don't spoil my day.' I was instantly thrown off my balance because he was smiling, a sight I really was not used to. He waved when he saw me. I tried to do a natural smile but I know it was more of a grimace. And just when I felt what does this ogre want, he really threw me by saying how well the garden was doing and thanks for looking after the sheep and lambs. His manner made me even more suspicious. He wandered around the garden and actually approved of the way it was all looking. He said he had come to have a look at the attic again as the chap he sent to inspect it said he couldn't find any sign of a leak, so it was all a bit mysterious. I said there was still a damp patch on the ceiling and suggested as the front door was open, he go and have a look. I thought It was best I kept myself out of the way and leave him to it.

It wasn't long before he emerged from the croft and said he was going into the loft to find out for himself, I watched him climb up the ladder and disappear into the roof space, I knew he would find nothing wrong with the roof, it was all about Alice and no-way was I ever going to mention it to him again, I can still remember the last time. Sure, enough after ten minutes he was back down in the garden looking puzzled. He said he would arrange for the roof to be re-sealed as obviously there was a leak somewhere and he added it often happened in buildings of this age, time made the oak timbers shrink and cause cracks in the walls and also the foundations. I asked how old the croft was, he replied he wasn't sure but it was built long before the farmhouse which was two hundred years old. He also added that he would send someone to clear out all the rubbish in the loft before the builders came as there was hardly any room to move up there, again he unnerved be by apologising for all the inconvenience it had and would cause me. I just smiled, and then he asked me would I like to move out whilst the work was being carried out, before I had time to reply, he said he had a small barn conversion on the farm that I would be welcome to use as it would be noisy and messy once the builders started. I really did not have much time to consider it and all I could think of was the bees and the garden. I thanked him and said I would be okay and I did not want to leave the garden, as it was a busy time. He smiled again, which I am starting to find unsettling and said it was only a short drive from the farm to here each day. For a moment I was dumbstruck and did not want to make any more excuses and then he said don't worry if I changed my mind then the barn would be there and if I got time to pop up and have a look, as I would be surprised how much nicer it was than the croft. I almost got caught up in his generosity and only just stopped myself from thanking him for being so nice to me. He waved goodbye and left me slightly bewildered as to whom I had just met.

I know one thing for sure I really must get up into the attic before the builders come and throw out any evidence of Alice's existence, my knees are nearly healed and I know I can now manage the steep ladder. Half of me is excited and the other half is afraid of what I might unleash as her visits seem to have stopped, I really don't want to disturb her.

After Simon's visit my mind was really not on my gardening and as I have an ever-growing list of things I need, I have decided I am going to the village. I mainly want to visit the quaint hardware shop with the equally quaint proprietor, top of my list is some form of cloche to keep the young plants warm and some form of netting to deter the rabbits from eating the young plants. I am not an avid gardener and am not trying too hard to stop nature, I really enjoy the wildlife they are great company and I would not begrudge sharing my produce with them, everything living has to eat.

Throughout the whole journey to the shops my mind was mulling over the conversation with my landlord. I thought what harm would it do to look at the barn he offered me, after all I had nothing to lose and if the building work was as bad as he insinuated then I would not hesitate to move out.

I parked the van easily right outside the hardware shop and marvelled at the amount of merchandise they had managed to put outside the shop on the pavement, it took me back to my childhood when there was no online shopping and you had to trail through the high street for all your groceries, usually a very looked forward to Saturday afternoon, carrying everything in shopping bags and my mother pulling a tartan trolley on wheels that she had to lift onto the bus, dad never came as all men were at home on a Saturday afternoon watching the football match and checking their pools.

The bell on the door jangled as I entered the shop, a signal for the shopkeeper to rush from the back room and ask what he could do for me. All I really wanted was to have a wander around the aladdins cave which was full to overflowing of everything you could possibly ever need for the home or garden. I asked for cloches and he said what did I need them for and then followed with a long informative conversation about the benefits of polythene with metal supports or rigid plastic without supports, I settled for rigid plastic. Next on my list was netting, who would believe it came in so many gauges, lengths, widths, colours and weights, I settled for whatever he thought I should have. I left with everything I needed and lots of extra advice on growing vegetables and an exceptionally kind offer of visiting the garden and seeing how I was getting on. I declined for the moment and thanked him for his help. I left as I could feel my claustrophobia panic button was being pressed, no fault of the kind man purely my mental instability that catches me out when I feel trapped. I quickly packed my purchases into the van and sat for a while, wondering if I should go straight back home or wait a little while, calm down and continue looking around the rest of the shops.

Just when I think I am coping well on my own, something happens and I want to run and run, why, I have no idea but it trips me up when I least expect it. I feel quite deflated now and a wave of grief washes over me and the old feelings of reality make my mood sink into a grey place, not as black as it used to be. The feeling fleets and subsides, as my attention is caught by seeing Rob coming out of the post office, he sees me and waves, smiling he ambles over to the van. I wind the window down and instantly my fears drop away. For some reason I am really pleased to see him. He looks at the back seat and comments on my purchases, and then says he is just going for a beer how about joining him as I owe him a pint as I deserted him last time, he invited me out. I surprised myself and accepted, I locked the van and followed him down an alley beside the church hall and was pleasantly surprised when we came across a small stone built public house with a small garden that backed onto a running stream. He chose a bench seat and table near the water and pointed out that it was a trout stream and if I watched closely, I would see the fish hiding in the reeds of the fast-flowing water. I gave him a ten-pound note and he went off to get drinks. I felt strangely odd sitting there and then realised I was feeling guilty about having a drink with a man, what would Luca say if he knew. For goodness sake where do all these thoughts come from, my husband is dead.

 We sat in the garden for almost an hour, we chatted about music and bees, well mainly music, it seemed I hadn't heard of any of the folk bands that he was talking about. I tried to join in with conversation about the music I liked, but it fell on deaf ears and he said that Martin J Jay was making a guest appearance at the Barn, which left me completely unimpressed, I tried to look enthusiastic but he saw through my falseness, he said, he was going to make sure I would grow to like the folk scene and he was going to treat me as a challenge. Obviously, he didn't know me that well, and I said, I hoped he was a good loser, that seemed to make him more determined to prove to me how he could persuade me to like his music. I tried to change the subject and talk about the croft and the leak in the roof and how I had been offered a barn on the farm whilst it was being done. He thought I should make the most of the offer and use it, as he'd seen it and thought it was much more comfortable than the croft. I asked him about Simon, and mentioned that they had been at school together, he said they were good mates and Simon had been lucky enough to go to the mainland to university, but unlike Simon he had failed miserably at school and had made a living with his father on the islands doing a bit of this and that. He mentioned that Simon had married a girl he brought back to the island with him when he left university and became a lecturer, and then he progressed and opened a publishing house, before he became an author of travel books. I think I sounded a little bit too interested in Simon Blake and Rob went on to tell me how Simon was born lucky and had never had to worry about money and didn't know what hard graft was as he had staff to do all the dirty work. I sensed a lot of resentment. Foolishly I said he most probably had to work really hard to get through university as I had done that myself and I found it really stressful and that was exactly how I had met my husband. He then sat hunched over his beer appearing to be deep in thought, we seemed to have hit a silent moment and I started to feel uncomfortable, it was time for me to return to the solitude of my sad but uncomplicated life.

Somehow the edge had been taken off the afternoon, I thanked Rob for the drink and said I would most probably give the folk night a miss and would phone him if I changed my mind, then stupidly added, come by for coffee sometime, regretting it as soon as the words left my careless mouth.

Strangely enough I think the afternoon was a little tense but I still enjoyed it, it was a baby step forward. I still have mixed feelings about being happy, I think that is normal.

I had a pleasant drive back to the croft, occasionally stopping to look at the everchanging colours of the hills and the vast sky tumbling above me. I seemed to have had quite an eventful day, lots to think about. I unloaded my supplies and stacked them in the garden, something caught my eye, it was the bees, they had left the hive and had gathered in the apple tree creating a heaving buzzing mess. This was the last thing I needed, I had to remember what to do, I found my bee mask and a cardboard box small enough to gather them. I was more worried to why they had decided to leave. I checked the hive the queen was still there but somehow a large piece of cotton fabric had been stuffed into the front, blocking the entrance, no wonder they were upset. It took a while to move them and convince them to return to the hive, quite a few flew back to their home as soon as I disturbed them and a few decided to stay in the tree until I went indoors. Once inside I pulled the fabric out of my pocket it was a long strip of filthy rag, who could have done such a thing and then the blood in my veins froze as I looked more closely at the scrap, little white embroidered daisies stood out on a faded blue background. The fabric was real not a figment of my imagination, I am so tired of this mystery person, what in heavens name happened to her and where is she. I really will have to concentrate on finding Alice or going completely insane, I will have to decide which one will it be.

YOU CANNOT HAVE A RAINBOW WITHOUT RAIN.

Tomorrow the attic of the croft is being cleared, ready for the new roof. A large skip has been delivered and this afternoon I am going up to the farm to look at the barn Simon offered me. Time is running out for me to have a good look up in the attic, so today is the last chance I will have. As I climb up into the darkness I feel like a naughty child, doing something that they are forbidden to do, I really am trespassing especially after I have been warned to keep out by the landlord, well I owe it to Alice.

What a mess, there must be years of rubbish up here, the dust irritates my nostrils. I have bought my torch and warily shine it into the dark corners hoping not to see anything untoward. I can feel my heart beating as I pull an old rug from under the eaves, what did I expect to find, perhaps a body wrapped in it, nothing just backing, the moths had long ago eaten any pattern. Again, I hesitantly tugged at a great heap of tarpaulin, it covered an even greater crumpled pile, no body, just dust, and then my foot stepped on something so uneven I thought I would fall headlong into the darkness. I shone my torch down to my feet and there it was, a thick rusty chain, it was so heavy, my heart raced as I pulled and tugged, it wouldn't budge. I don't know what I expected, but I just stopped myself from running down that ladder not wanting to find out what was on the other end. I moved an old tin trunk and piles of frayed heavy rope and then came to part of the chain wrapped around the roof beam, it trailed off further, under more dusty boxes, finally I reached the end, my emotions that I only just kept under the surface, broke through my delicate shield and I sunk to my knees clutching a rusty ankle manacle, so sad, so real, and to no surprise, when I moved the evil fetter the floor beneath it is soaking wet, just as Alice mentioned in her sad journal. As I stood there the whole building shuddered and seemed to sigh. Alice was not up here, once she had been, that I do know. I left the revolting chain in place where it lay, a sickening reminder of a poor girls last terrifying days on this earth, it left me with a heavy feeling in every limb of my body. I shakily climbed down the ladder and half expected her to be watching me, she wasn't, the orchard was normal, the sheep were nursing their lambs, the bees had calmed down, nothing had changed, only me, I have changed.

Before I leave for the visit to the farm I have put Alice's notebook from the loft in my pocket, I am now prepared to tell Simon about his ancestors writing and what I have found today, I am determined not to be ridiculed or intimidated by this man, my journey through grief has made me at times weak and pathetic but the, 'Time will heal,' saying might be truer than I really believe, I am strong and from now on no-one will ever suggest that through my grief I have become mentally unstable, Alice was real and she deserves better.

As I leave, I notice the pair of Ravens are raiding the garden for nesting materials, they seem to have grown quite used to me and just fluff up their feathers when they see me, I can see I will have to make a scarecrow before long. I still feel a little jittery inside as I drive up to Weathercote farm, I am interested in seeing the barn but forefront in my mind is Alice and justice for her.

Betty opens the gate for me and says that Tom will meet me up in the courtyard. It is quite surprising to see the place in daylight, it all looks so different. The courtyard is much larger than I imagined and I can see evidence of work being carried out on the cobbles, the farmhouse is quite magnificent. Tom emerges from the house and points to an area for me to park. I can see across the yard that a stable/barn has been converted, it looks invitingly attractive with window boxes and a small patio at the front edged with earthenware pots containing colourful spring flowers. Tom greets me and opens the barn door, I must say my first impression was surprising, shiny oak floors, and an open plan ground floor, inside the ceiling was so high, with exposed rafters and a small door high up in the roof which Tom informed me was an owl door. It was all so light and airy and I thought how nice it would have been if the croft had been renovated the same way. I followed Tom around all the rooms and we settled in the beautiful kitchen which overlooked the fields and hills, that I have come to know so well. Tom said I would be daft to not take it on as the croft was going to be wrecked and after the roof was sorted the whole place was going to be modernised, I said that was news to me, I thought Simon said it was just the roof being repaired. He assured me that his boss had decided to renovate it after I had complained about the windows not fitting, the roof leaking and the walls crumbling and added that the croft had started to become a liability, especially as it was rented out to the public, who could sue him at any time. I suddenly realised to my landlord, I am just a paying customer, just the public. I was fuming, Tom was quite apologetic and thought that I knew the tenancy was coming to an end, and as the croft had become quite inhabitable it wasn't viable to have a tenant, he added that as his boss was most probably going to live abroad for a while, he had suggested that eventually he might put all the smaller buildings on the estate up for sale, as his sister who had an equal share in the estate wanted her money out of the business. My mind was racing ahead, what about my bees, the garden and of course Alice, how could that man come to see me and not mention a word to me about having to leave. I suspect he was ging to let his agent do the dirty work. I am so angry I feel the demons inside me reach for a gun and put the man out of my misery. Blinded by anger I leave and walk to my car afraid of what I might do if I see Simon, as I pull open the van door, the very man himself walks across the yard looking so pleased with himself. I wind my window down and give him my complete vocabulary of choice words and swear to him that this will not be the last he will hear from me.

Shocked was not an expression I would describe he had on his face, when I reversed over the clay pots edging the patio, the crunching sound was deafening, in my mirror I saw him talking to Tom and rubbing his hand through his hair. I didn't stop shaking until I arrived at the croft, and then I cried for everything, Luca, Mother, Alice, my bees and me, I shoved the door so hard the hinges screamed. Inside I stood for an age trying to think what to do next, I think I can only blame myself; this would never have happened if I hadn't complained so much about the state of the croft. I felt in my pocket and took out Alice's notebook, I so wanted to help her but in my pursuits all I managed to do was get myself evicted by a man who hadn't got the guts to tell me to my face.

The weather changed to go with my mood, grey clouds rolled in from the sea and white foam crashed upon the shore, the sea birds caught in the gusty wind flew sideways trying to land. The Ravens up on the roof did a flying display defying the weather, swooping down and cawing loudly, I will miss this all so much if I have to leave.

After a fretful few hours feeling angry and then sorry for myself, I have thought of a way I can stay, I have a plan. I will engage, Vittori Investments and my solicitor in London to make Simon Blake an offer for the croft, an offer he can't refuse, I will buy it with all the faults, also the offer could save him a lot of expense and trouble. I don't want him to know it is me, as I am sure he would never consider the proposal.

I tried to send an e-mail to London but as usual the signal is intermittent, the same goes for my mobile. I don my anorak and brave the wind and walk up the hill until I see the signal on my mobile is awake. The phone rings for ages and eventually an answer phone politely asks me to leave a message and someone will get back to me as soon as the office is open. Of course, these people in high salaried jobs go home at a reasonable time, I leave a clear message with all the details and say I will follow up the message with an e-mail which I do outlining the exact offer I want to make and instructing them to get back to me as soon as possible.

Sleep did not come easy, I watched the moon rise over the hills and slowly wander across the night sky, moving in and out of the thick rain clouds, somewhere up on the moorland a fox screamed and pierced the silence. My mind was mulling over so many things and nothing seemed to make any sense, eventually I got up and looked out of the window at the sea, I could just make out the reflection of the moon on the water creating a shimmering pathway right up to the beach. I forced the stiff window open and smelt the sea air, which is much stronger at night, a mixture of seaweed and ozone, if only you could bottle that aroma. I tried to still my mind which was completely in overdrive, I must look at what is real and not worry about things I can do nothing about, as always when things go wrong Luca is not here to sort it out or to tell me to calm down and not be so dramatic. I think what he would say to me in this situation and I hear his strong comforting voice say, 'None of this matters, it is all material, people are the only things that really matter, everything else is replaceable.' I had forgotten what his voice sounded like, I looked behind me, fully expecting to find him standing in the room. 'Oh Luca, I miss you so much, why did you leave me without a goodbye. I'm so useless without you.'

I think in the grim light of day that everything has become too much for me and I have obsessed about Alice and it has done me no good at coping with my loss, I have treated her as a distraction from thinking about the nightmare that was going on in my head, and I believe I have purposely centered my anger about Luca leaving me onto Simon Blake. I have been here a while now and become too involved in this place, it was supposed to be a sanctuary where I could come to grips with who I am.

I have phoned Rob to collect the Bees and hives, nothing else matters the plants will grow as sure as the sun rises every-day. I have started to collect my bits together and luckily, I had flattened the packing boxes and kept them, I am so glad that I have made this decision to have a break from all this, and for a moment, I also wonder if I have been too hasty in trying to buy the croft, Tom was really quite wrong, my tenancy was not up, I have paid the rent for a year but in the scheme of things it is just money and Simon Blake needs it more than me. Peace of mind is more important. I have no need to let anyone know here, I told Rob that I wasn't getting on with the bees and had changed my mind about beekeeping, as usual he was laid back and casual about it and said if I cooked him brunch on Saturday morning then he would come and get them, and he asked had I changed my mind about Saturday night's folk evening, I didn't answer.

A lorry has just delivered a skip right outside the gate and without a word the driver dumped it and drove off, I really have become invisible, something I always knew would happen. Not long after the arrival of the skip a builder's truck rumbled down the road carrying great crates of stone roofing tiles and plastic sacks of sand and cement, again they placed them right outside the gate making it difficult to get past them, I didn't waste my breath asking them to move them out of the way as I knew what the answer

would be. Really none of this is anything to do with me it's not my property, I fully expect the builders to arrive at any moment.

I feel a bit like a nomad, I don't really know where I want to be and feel I will just keep searching for something that I now understand, I will never ever find, as it doesn't actually exist. Sometime I have to book the ferries, I will leave that until I decide when I will be ready to leave, it shouldn't take too long as I didn't bring that much with me. I will really miss this place as it is so beautiful but, I need some security where I can feel settled and safe.

Just as I expected a rickety white van arrived just before lunch today and a comedy duo rolled up at the door. The older of the two informed me he and his son were going to mend the roof and would try not to be too noisy as the owner said that I had refused to leave so they would have to work around me and then added with a big grin on his face that they were also warned that I could be a bit spiky and to keep out of my way. Before I could defend myself, he also added that he told the boss not to worry as they could handle themselves. I couldn't think of a reply, so offered them a cup of coffee before they made a start, that I suspect will not be today, they both preferred sweet tea, the father nudged his son as I walked away and commented, 'See I told you I could handle her, she'll be eating out of my hand before you know it.' 'I can hear you, I'm not deaf,' I quickly retorted. I returned with the tea in two large mugs that were perfect for builder's tea. I left them to their survey, and went to pack a few more boxes.

It was mid-afternoon when Simon came to visit the builders, I heard his Land Rover pull up outside, at first, I really wanted to have another go at him for telling the builders I was difficult, but I think I have made my decision and what is the point of causing any more stress unless I really have to. I grabbed my coat and my phone and put my earplugs in and made for the beach, and left them to it. I took my usual path down to the beach, this shoreline and all the wildlife it offers is something I will dearly miss, it has been a saviour to me on some of my saddest days. The wind still blows across the bay and as it is still only late spring it has a chill to it, I zip up my jacket and pull the hood over my head, I walk along the familiar stretch of beach and can't help but think of Alice, she must have played on this sand and paddled in this sea, most probably collected shells and sea glass and threaded hag stones. As I walk, I can see an outline in the sand, someone has drawn a heart, it must have been about ten feet wide, an arrow was drawn through the middle and to my surprise the name Alice was written in the heart. How odd, now what was I going to make of this. My mind really was so tired, that I didn't want to have to analyse any more weird things concerning Alice Blake, another time I would have been so eager, now is different, I have to believe it has all been just a set of coincidences put together by my me to take my mind off my loss.

I walk further and feel the wind getting stronger, I

turn my back to the squall and instantly I am warmer. Ahead of me I can see the outline of a figure, I hope it is someone just walking their dog, as I grow nearer, I realise who it is and brace myself for another round. He waves as I approach and I inadvertently wave back, his collar is turned up and his long hair is blowing over his face obscuring his mood. I quickly remember the crushed pots and feel even though I don't want to, I should offer to pay for them.

I take a deep breath, I look up at him, he seems a lot taller when you get nearer. He opens his mouth; the wind whips his words away and they are lost in the breeze I signal to him I can't hear a word and he takes my arm and guides me to a niche in the rocks. The crashing noise instantly stops and I feel my hair that has been standing on end relax and shroud my face in a tangled mess. He is standing far too close to me and I cannot move any further away from him without tripping, I feel uncomfortable and awkward as he is invading my space, he realises this and steps back. 'I think we have to talk. Firstly, I am so sorry about the croft, I think Tom got hold of the wrong stick, anything I mentioned about selling the croft was for the future not now.' I didn't believe a word he was saying. 'I only offered you the barn as I thought the disruption would be too much mess and noise for you. And it was only a suggestion that it might be a good idea to renovate the rest once the weather got warmer, I can understand how you felt and I can only apologies.' Oh, damn I preferred it when he was arrogant, I can't cope with him being human. For the first time I wasn't looking at him through a red haze. I thought I should apologies for the pots and offered to pay for them. He refused and said he also had to apologies for his comments he made when I told him about his ancestor Alice, he said he found it difficult to understand anything supernatural but, should not have said what he did. As I have said before, I can't handle anyone being too kind to me, I turned away so frightened of him seeing my weakness. And then to stop the flood that I thought would ensue if I didn't change the subject I said, I know you don't believe me but, before I leave, I have found some things about Alice Blake that I feel you should know about, please bear with me and when I am gone you can think what you will of me. His face changed as I pushed past him ready to make a swift exit from this situation, I braced the wind and wearily walked along the sand, he caught me up and stood in front of me. 'Alright, obviously this is all really important to you, I want to hear what you have to say, and what did you say about leaving.' I took another deep breath but really did not want to talk anymore, I told him I only came here to get over the loss of my husband and mother and it was mistake and had not been the answer I was looking for and I had decided it was best for me to return to London. He didn't say a word, politely I suggested that if he was remotely interested in the information about his ancestor then let me know and I would give him the notebook and locket, he asked if he could have my mobile number and said he would call me, I said as I was always here, he could just come by, of course after he had consulted his diary. The last thing I wanted was him having my telephone number.

The builders were still at the croft and had unpacked some of the roof stones and stacked them against the wall on top of my runner beans, Simon looked at the crushed mess. I said never mind none of it mattered now. He asked me about the bees, I told him Rob was coming on Saturday to pick them up, I sagged for a moment and was suddenly so tired I could hardly stand and stumbled slightly, I made an excuse to go indoors, he asked if I was okay, I mumbled 'fine,' and was so relieved to reach the door, I slumped down on the couch. I closed my eyes and slept fully clothed for the next eight hours, waking in the early hours wondering why I had all my clothes on. I felt so fatigued and put it down to stress, this has been another strange year, I hope I will feel more normal when I get back home, even though I am not sure what my normal is these days.

Now I have made my mind up about leaving, I feel quite relieved, I won't have any trouble finding somewhere to live in London, my own house is leased until the end of the year, which I don't mind at all, all the memories will still be there, along with all my treasures, safely stored in the loft. Even though time has soothed the intense pain of loss, I will never forget my life with my family and fully understand, that they are in one place and I am in another. I haven't told any friends yet that I am returning, I wonder whether to, or just pick up with them once I have found somewhere to live. I am sure most of them have moved on, occasionally I have sent the odd text message to some of my close friends, everything is different when you are a single woman with married friends. Being a widow puts you in a very different social position.

I am so glad when the builder and his son shout, 'Goodbye Mrs.,' and leave, they work really hard but their radio blasts all day long, and they sing badly to all the songs, my mind is full of bad nineties music, that I catch myself singing along to. I wave vigorously from the door as the rickety van disappears from view, so pleased the banging and crashing has stopped along with the vocal entertainment.

The change to summertime is really making a difference now and the evenings are starting to get a little lighter, which allows for a walk before closing the curtains to the night sky. I have at last found the stream where the otters are and I am truly fascinated by their behaviour, I could sit for hours and watch them, these are something I will miss, but if I am lucky enough to buy this place then I will one day return when things will be easier even if I only use it as a holiday home.

I take my familiar walk up to the top of the hill passing the ruins, I walk halfway across the top of the peak and climb over a stile, I journey downwards, I reach an open area where I can see the stream meandering through the hollow of the fields below, a beautifully sheltered spot ideal for a moment of solitude. On my way down the rocky path, I can already see the long slender bodies of the otters, the colour of chocolate, gracefully gliding low in the water, they swim silently making a V bow wave, already they have chosen their partners and hopefully will produce young in the summer months, they are magical to watch and great time wasters, time passes quickly when your mind is occupied especially by creatures so amusing. The banks of this river are so natural and untouched by man, it is a haven for wildlife, plenty of trees and vegetation, many places for the otters to lie up in the day without any interruptions. The light is changing and I quietly leave the stream and journey back up through the trees and across the field, a fox runs in front of me startled at seeing me, as if my magic he fades into the shadows, I am sure he is watching and waiting for me to leave his territory, I have interrupted his hunting. I reach the stile just in time to see the sun dropping down over the horizon, the glow it casts is unreal and reminds me of the old master's paintings of the heavens, where a golden glow comes from underneath the clouds, the only thing missing is the band of Holy angels playing their heavenly harps. The ruins cast long shadows, I watch the landscape change and the air becomes cooler as the night sky rolls in. From this height I can see the croft far below and I pause for a moment to look at what could be mine one day, a thrill runs through my body. Even though I am leaving to gather myself together, I really love this place, but I will not miss having a landlord, something that has been quite new to me and a difficult experience, even though on second thoughts I think I might have been a difficult tenant. The croft is shrouded in a blue tarpaulin and looks even sadder than it did before, I am glad to be leaving and letting the builders get on with all the works, planned, if it is put up for sale at least it will have been renovated and little will need to be done. I unlock the door with the giant iron key and smile at the screaming hinges and think it will be such a shame to lose some of the character of the place.

This morning the sun rose early and the sky is a vast ceiling of pure azure blue, looks to be the start of a perfect day, even though I am leaving I have continued to tend the garden, which is slowly reverting back to the wild, just about every pest has been informed that I am leaving a garden full of mouth-watering snacks, even the big fat purple and grey wood pigeons that have escaped the hunters, are blatantly devouring the new shoots in the vegetable patch, in front of my very eyes. Rob should be coming to collect the bees this morning, I hope they get used to another place. I have nearly finished packing the boxes and have just left out the things I need, I have booked my ferry tickets and I shall be out of here in a weeks' time, since I have made up my mind about returning to London, I seem to be less stressed, I think because I have had so much to think about. I still have heard nothing from my solicitor about the croft, I presume as it's not on the market yet, he will have to approach the agent, I suppose it could all take a while to sort out and even then, it might not be for sale. Whatever happens, it will be meant for some strange reason.

I have been waiting all morning now for Rob to arrive, I have texted him twice and tried to phone him, I am not going to wait any longer as I don't want to waste the rest of the day as I want to take my camera out and try to capture the essence of the island before I leave.

The sun is really sweltering, which is such a bonus when it is still only springtime. This is the first time since I have been here that I have been able to leave my coat off, even my Aran jumper is starting to feel a little warm and clingy. The tide is far out and the sand is still moist, I leave my shoes on the shingle and roll up my jeans to my knees, my bare feet squelch leaving perfect footprints in the sand, comforting cool water oozes between my toes as I paddle in the edge of the ebbing tide. I take photographs of the view behind me on the land and the high rocks that tower above the beach, my feet trail along the shoreline, I remove my sweater and tie it around my waist. As I reach the edge of the bay, I come across amazing rock pools that hold so much life, the stones around them are moulded into strange shapes by the limpets and sea weed that has draped itself over the rocks like a wet green blanket. Little green crabs scurry sideways at the bottom of the pool, using their giant claw to sift through the shingle. Each pool holds different forms of wildlife and I discover soft bodied starfish, each body resembling a small piece of intricate beaded artwork, how can nature create something so beautiful. I could spend many hours searching the pools for anything that moves. The sun is really pitching and I make for the shelter of the caves, first remembering when the high tide will occur, I really don't want to spend the rest of the day stuck here. Instantly the temperature drops as the air becomes almost icy, I adjust my eyes to the darkness, looking up I can see the ceiling is really high and the passage is wide enough for me to pass through without feeling claustrophobic. The air is so easy to breathe and the coolness causes my skin to tingle with goose-bumps, I wonder where the tunnel leads to, it's obviously man made, perhaps something to do with mining or smugglers. I am a little apprehensive of going too far inside and keep looking back at the light coming from the entrance, I wish I had bought a torch, there is something in the middle of the passage and I hesitate for a moment in case it moves. I can feel my heart thumping inside my chest but still my legs keep walking. I laugh to myself when I reach a block of stone which has been carved out to form a bowl, in the semi-darkness I can just see the shimmer of water, I think this is some sort of holy well or pagan font, the water is cold and as I stand looking about the small chamber, I can see the remains of candles sitting in niches around the walls. I refrain from going any further, even though the cave is fascinating, I decide to leave in case I've disturbed some ancient site, it's always the way, I have found something I would really like to find out more about and I am leaving soon. Perhaps I will return, who knows.

The sun is even hotter when I emerge and is blinding after the darkness of the caves, my pockets are full of shells and stones and a beautiful long white feather that I picked up, which I presume came from the large Herring gulls that spend so much time on the beach.

Over the first year after Luca died, I nearly filled a coffee jar with white feathers, just after the funeral there was one on the bonnet of the car and from then on, I saw them floating down in front of me, at the shops, in the garden, once I chased one across a busy road before it landed in a puddle, I was so desperate for a message from the angels, Luca would have said that some bird was up in a tree preening and had pulled them out on purpose. He was stable and down to earth and kept my butterfly mind perfectly grounded. Sadly, now I am free to run with the wind and all the headless chickens and am not grounded at all, I am free to make all my decisions but spend a lot of time making the wrong ones.

My mind is daydreaming as I walk back up the path to the croft, I am watching small white puffy clouds drift across the sky when my phone startles me, it's such an unusual occurrence for it to ring. I can see that its Rob, and about time, he is his usual jaunty self and apologises for not calling me sooner, apparently, he overslept this morning and has only just seen all his messages, he says it's a good thing really, because he had realised it's best to move the bees at night, when they are quieter and all gathered inside their hives. I agree with him, he added he's playing at the barn tonight and am I sure I don't want to go. I assure him I haven't changed my mind but thanks for the offer, he says he will come tomorrow evening as long as I am really sure I want to get rid of them. I assure him I am absolutely positive and then I mention that I am leaving the island and returning to London. He thought I was really stupid going back to that awful place and asked why, I just said I had stayed far too long and it was time to leave.

The sun is still shining strongly, I throw all the windows open, how different everything is in the sunshine, I can see all the cobwebs in the corners and understand that the place really does need some attention. This afternoon I have decided to take a break from packing and go up to the farm shop and find something tasty for my supper, Betty is sure to have something delicious made up. I am just leaving when I see the builders truck coming down the road, I am sure they said they wouldn't be working over the weekend, I am already in my van so I decide to keep going, they can easily carry on without me. I wind my window down as we pass, they are not going to do any work, but need some of their tools that they left in the loft for a job they are doing this afternoon. I just stop long enough to hear why they are here and before they can go into their comedy act, I put my foot down and drive up the hill.

When I enter the farm shop Betty is smiling as usual, instantly she tells me all the things that she has made and how good they are and proceeds to show me. She says they are so sorry that I am leaving and Tom feels he's to blame, I assure her he's not it is all my decision, she asks is it because I don't like the place, I tell her nothing can be further from the truth I find the island the most beautiful place I have ever stayed. I mentioned that one day I might come back, who knows. I buy a fresh salmon and prawn parcel and a jar of homemade hollandaise sauce to go with it and a bunch of watercress that is crisp and fresh, and then as usual when I come into the shop, I fill my basket, I add elderflower wine made locally, delicious strawberry and champagne preserve, a fresh lemon meringue tart, four beef sausages and a round of black-pudding, adding a punnet of button mushrooms and six enormous hens' eggs. Betty suggests I should really buy some of the farms cured bacon, I think about the little piglets I have seen running through the yard and decline her offer. As I leave, I see the builders pulling up into the shop's carpark, they don't look their usual jovial selves, very soon I find out why. Apparently when they went up into the loft to retrieve their tools the whole place had been trashed, their ladders had been reduced to piles of wood and their overalls were shredded and paint had been splashed over all their power tools and the ones that weren't ruined were thrown into the orchard and the tool box had disappeared completely, they were furious and wanted to know what I knew about it. I was so shocked and explained I had only just left the croft; someone must have done it whilst I was away. They said you couldn't make that sort of mess in such a short time; it would have taken a strong person to move it all to the orchard. I assured them when I checked on the bees this morning there was no sign of anything untoward. I don't think for one minute they believed me and I had a slight suspicion they thought I was somehow to blame. Betty heard everything they said and she offered to fetch Simon to sort it out, I couldn't think of anything to say apart from I was at a loss to explain what could have happened. I gathered my shopping and said I was going back home to check if anyone had been in the croft. They didn't seem keen on me leaving and wanted me to wait and talk to Simon, I just left eager to see for myself.

I don't remember the journey back to the croft as I was so worried to what I might find, one thing is for sure everything was intact when I left. I parked the van and hurried indoors, anticipating the worst, nothing, it was just as I thought it would be, I checked the drawers, nothing had changed, I went outside intent on climbing the ladder and checking the attic, it was then that I saw her, and smelt the putrid acrid aroma of death that permeated my saddened soul. Alice had decayed barely beyond recognition; her face was skeletal and her fine full cheeks were now leathered and sunken over her partly exposed bones. Her eyes were hooded and sunken and had faded, almost opaque, her shoulders were piercing through the thin soiled fabric of her once blue dress. She stepped toward me and I recoiled from her she reached out a skeletal hand to me, a small hand of a child, a claw with skin peeling and hanging in shreds. The horror of the situation was a living nightmare, she moved forward again, and then the scream, an unearthly sound, which haunts me to this day, a scream that pierced my eardrums and didn't stop. Her distorted mouth opened so wide that it cracked the bones in her jaw and still she screamed in absolute terror.

'Help me, Help me, Help me.'

Over and over, she repeated the same words, becoming louder and louder, I covered my ears, but the shrill scream penetrated my brain, I thought my head would explode. Rooted to the ground, my leaden feet refused to move, I wanted to get away from this horrendous sight and run indoors to safety, still she screamed and screamed. I am not sure how long I stayed there with Alice, then slowly everything around me changed, and strangely I found myself in the loft, witnessing a small figure curled up helplessly, lying on a filth ridden carpet. In the dim light the only sounds I could hear was a quiet sob escaping from the emancipated small body dying in front of me, and a constant drip, drip, drip, coming from the broken skylight window, high above me in the roof. Alice's thin fingers rested on a notebook, the one I had recently found, in the attic, the only difference between them being, this one was new and not old and faded. It was all so real, I don't know how long I was up there, but I witnessed the moment the sobbing stopped, and then something touching me made me look down, a dog, a black and white collie was licking my hand, I couldn't look away, and eventually when I did, Alice had gone, and I was back in the garden, confusingly the dog was still at my side and then I noticed my landlord walking towards me holding a dog's lead, he called for it to heel and the dog obediently obeyed its master. I must have been in shock as at first, I couldn't make out what Simon was saying, and then he asked me again, he wanted to know who I was talking to when he drove down the lane and where did she go. And added was I alright as I looked as though I had seen a ghost. I couldn't reply or string a sentence together. I looked around the orchard, nothing, no Alice, no tools laying around, and then I saw it, a blue piece of faded fabric draped on the pile of roof stones stacked against the wall. I picked it up and told Simon I was so glad he had seen me talking to someone, because I was pretty sure she was his ancestor Alice, that had disappeared long ago and I thought her remains were most probably here somewhere. He obviously didn't believe me and marched off looking around the garden and then the beach and up to the rocks, nothing. He looked quite serious and I could tell he thought I was completely bonkers and was not sure how to handle me. He said we must talk about it soon, and the reason he had come to see me was the builders had made a complaint about their tools and the state of the attic. He paused for a moment apprehensive to ask me if I knew anything about it. I shrugged my shoulders and walked wearily back indoors. He didn't follow me and the last I saw of him was the back of him climbing up the ladder to the attic, his dog followed me indoors and sat beside me with his head on my lap. Fifteen minutes later Simon knocked quietly on the half open door. He said that it appeared we'd had a visit from vandals, they had trashed the loft and destroyed a lot of the builders' tools and emptied bags of cement and paint out over everything, he assured me he did not think I was responsible for any of it, and did I know that all the bees had gone, and there was no evidence of any of the hives being used. I was stunned by all that had happened today, I said I saw the bees this morning and they were okay. I told him Rob was coming to collect them this evening. He said that he remembered it was the music night at the barn and wondered was I going, he seemed a little subdued, I told him I wasn't going as I still had a lot of packing to do, I paused thinking as to whether I should mention the things I found in the loft. He was standing looking at me, as if he didn't know what to say next, I asked him to not lose his cool, but I had been up in the loft, even though, I knew he had told me not to, but after all the strange happenings I had to find out what was up there, then, I told him I wanted to give him the things that I found as I thought he should have them. I gave him the notebook, and tried to explain, what I had seen in the loft, not just the notebook but, the manacles and the old carpet, and I suggested before he judged me again, to read Alice's words. I opened the drawer and passed him the locket. He looked confused, and stared at the items as if they might burn his fingers. Completely changing the subject, he quietly uttered, that he thought in the light of the vandals it would be better if I stayed up at the barn until I left, just to be on the safe side. I declined his offer and said I would be alright, after all this had all been going on since I moved here, for the first time he said he wondered if it could possibly have anything to do with my name, and the likeness to his ancestor, I thought this was a break through to believing me, and then he found his normal sanctimonious voice, and asked had I read about her, in the old family book in the bookcase, and then perhaps put two and two together when I read the notebook, which could be just a young girls ramblings, he said in those days without television, people had to make up their own entertainment and this is most probably why she wrote what she did. He said she was definitely lost in the sea, and had I not seen her memorial stone up in the chapel graveyard, he said all the details of her death and the search for her were logged in the family bible, which he had up at the farm, and I was welcome to look go up and look at them. In fact, he said, 'Come on, let's go now, you look like you could do with a change of scenery,' I didn't really give it too much thought and followed him out to his car, the dog never left my side and kept nuzzling my hand, this did not go unnoticed. 'He's certainly taken a liking to you, it's unusual as he is not friendly at all these days, he was my late wife's dog.' As I sat in the front seat of the Range Rover, the dog insisted on licking the back of my neck. It didn't matter how many times Simon told Ghost off, the affection just carried on, his tail wagged constantly. Embarrassed, he said his wife had named the dog after her favourite film, he said after her death he had tried to call the dog a different name but he would only respond to Ghost.

On the short drive to the farm I thought about Simon, he must have gone through the same grief as I have done, everyone reacts to such sadness in different ways, it is so intimate and personal, but the loss is just the same. I didn't want to pry so I just said, I also liked the film and Ghost, was a good name for a dog.

Betty waved and looked surprised as we drove past the farm shop, through the gates and up the drive to Weathercote Farm. Somehow all my driving curiosity about Alice, seemed to have ebbed away and I was left with an overwhelming feeling of defeat.

Simon parked in the courtyard and opened the car door for me and the dog to climb out. Stepping into the house I could see it was a typical Shetland Farmhouse, it looked as though nothing had changed in a hundred years, no wonder that trees are scarce on this island, I presume they were all felled to build the beautiful beams and panels adorning the walls and ceilings. Even though the house was one of the biggest on the island, it felt cosy and warm. The entrance hallway had a welcoming fire in the grate and instantly Ghost laid down on the hearthrug in front of the welcoming warmth. Simon hung his coat in the downstairs cloakroom and offered to take mine, I was still cold so kept mine on. Betty must be kept busy here, the dark oak wooden floorboards had years of polish and elbow grease put into them, the wall lights reflected a golden glow in the gleaming boards. I was led through to the library, which also had a roaring fire in the large grate, and by the amount of papers on the desk I presumed this was Simon's office as well. I sank into a high-backed armchair beside the fire, amazed at the floor to ceiling lining of books. Simon disappeared muttering something about coffee, it seemed ages before he returned, as he did the thought came to me that this was the house that Alice must have grown up in, as a small child she most probably ran through the corridors and spied on her father in the library, her bedroom must have been upstairs and probably her nursery in the loft.

I cradled a steaming hot mug of coffee in my cold hands and just for a moment thought, what in heavens name am I doing here, this is not a place that I ever really wanted to be. Simon seemed unusually quiet and not his usual bombastic self. He set a small table in front of me and lifted a heavy book onto it. The family bible was an antique in its own right, it was leather bound in black stippled hide of some sort and embossed with gold leaf, that shone like sunbeams in the glow of the burning logs. He sat on the arm of my chair and turned the pages, finally coming to the inserts of births, deaths and marriages. There were beautifully decorated pages with drawings of angels and cherubs and writing in pen and ink describing, dates of birth and obituaries of the dead. He turned to the page for Alice, it gave her date of birth and sadly the date of her demise, presumed dead. In italic script it described her as a lively young girl who at times could be reckless, and that on that date in particular, she was seen by, George the stable boy near the rocks, down by the derelict fishing croft, he said she was standing near the edge and he told her to be careful. It went on to say, when at nightfall she didn't return a search party made up of local men was sent out to look for her, they found nothing, and the next morning, the body of her dog was found washed up on the beach. A month later a memorial service was held and a stone in her memory was erected in the churchyard on the estate.

My mind was racing trying to remember the name of the stable boy in Alice's notebook. Simon had not read the notes so he was confused as to what I was saying. I asked him for the journal and he said he had left it in the car and off he went to fetch it. He has said little since we arrived, and I have a suspicion that he thought once I read Alice's obituary in the bible, that I would let it all go. Quite a while passed before he returned and he had Betty with him. I understood immediately that he thought there would be safety in numbers, He said he thought Betty would better understand what I was saying as she knew all about the family matters. He handed the journal to Betty, made his apologies, and said that he had a prior engagement which he could not miss and left the room. I could tell Betty was not at the least interested in my findings and I made my excuses to take my leave. She tried to stop me saying he would only be half an hour and he had left her instructions to keep me here as he would give me a lift home. I opened the notebook and half-heartedly showed her the entry Alice had made about the men capturing her and the sad words she wrote in the loft, when no-one came to rescue her. Betty wanted to talk, but not about Alice, and then the questions began and I felt trapped. I left the notebook with her and thought if I didn't have it with me anymore, then perhaps Alice would leave me alone and haunt members of her own family. I am leaving in a few days and am glad to have a break from Alice Blake, I have enough on my mind regarding my own sad loss without, the demise of someone whom is no relation of mine. I walked the familiar trail across the fields, springtime was changing the whole landscape, likened to an artist washing the grey countryside with colour, even the wildlife was becoming braver and not hiding away in the daylight, they were ready to increase their families and gorge on the new spring grass that sprung from the yellowed turfs.

I arrived at the croft just as Rob was lifting the hives onto the back of his truck, a few stragglers were loose and frantically flying in circles, Rob said not to worry as they would follow the truck, and beside he didn't have far to go as Simon had phoned him about an hour ago and said he would have the hives in the farm orchard and look after them until you got back. I felt a little annoyed, I asked him why they should think I would be coming back. He was a little embarrassed and said, Simon knew I didn't really want to leave and had said, it would not be long before I returned. What a cheek. Of course, I couldn't tell Rob about my plan, to try and buy the place. I watched the truck leave and felt a little sad about the empty spot in the orchard.

I didn't feel like eating any of the delicious things that I had bought this morning, so much had happened since then. I felt in some way relieved that I had given the book and locket to Simon, it belonged to him after all regardless of who the owner was, they were found on his property.

I have tried to talk myself out of thinking too much about Alice anymore, because it is starting to disturb me, but I have a habit of not listening to myself and I know that before I leave this island, I must see her memorial, I find it hard to believe I have missed it, up there in the churchyard, that I have visited so often. I find myself reaching for my coat and pulling on my walking shoes. The night is crisp and cold and the clear sky is dotted with a million diamonds which reflect in the still ocean. I do not find the walk as comfortable as usual and suspect it's because I am leaving. It seems ages before I reach the rocks and the ruins of the church. I have my torch in my pocket and shine the light on the ancient graves, many of the inscriptions have long faded and the grave stones have tilted or fallen over. The torch flickers as I make my way through the long grass, there are no memorial stones to be found, I have never walked around this side of ruins as it is so overgrown and looks as though it has never been used for burials. I climb over broken fencing that nature has entwined with her own briars, my trousers catch on the brittle unkind thorns. As I look up, there in front of me, standing in all its magnificent glory, is the black silhouette of a stone angel, she is high on a plinth with her wings reaching up into the sky, her lifeless eyes are staring, looking out, beyond the beach, far across the ocean, such a fitting memorial for such a beloved child. Without even reading the lead inlaid inscription I know this is Alice's memorial, as I step closer my torch flickers again, in the starlight I can see, the Angel is surrounded by iron railings and it is quite impossible to get any closer. I wonder if she can be seen from the beach or do the rocks and trees conceal her. I am content to think that Alice has a fitting memorial, but I would have been happier to have found her resting place. Silently I say farewell to Alice Blake.

I take a slow walk back down to the croft, after such a strange day I am really surprised that nothing else has happened. I think about Simon and wonder if he will ever pick up that journal and if he does, will he read it.

I am so tired, what a day, I don't seem to have stopped to draw breath, I have just pulled off my socks and put my feet up on the footstall ready to toast my toes in front of the log burner, when I remember the last job I meant to do, before all the events of the day cluttered my butterfly mind, was to fill the firewood basket, which is now standing completely empty. I can barely see the last log I put on the fire and am annoyed that it will not last much longer. I hate the thought of spending the rest of the evening freezing, once the fire dies down the croft cools so quickly. Reluctantly I push myself to go out into the dark and fill the basket. As I open the door the north easterly wind envelopes me in a blanket of icy air, which goes right through me, freezing me to my very core, I stumble along the uneven path, that leads around to the side of the house, again just as I reach the lean-to the batteries on my torch decide to die. With my hands out in front of me I feel for the tarpaulin cover that is so ragged, it hardly protects the stack of wood leaning against the croft wall. My hands and feet are numb with the cold, I hate to think of all the creepy crawlies I can't see as I fill the basket, as I pick up the last log, I hesitate, I stop what I am doing, straining my senses, I can hear voices whispering, I listen, nothing, I must be imagining it, I turn to leave and the voices become slightly louder and fiercer, they are threatening and terrifying, I freeze unable to move, these are men's voices, I strain my ears to hear what they are saying. This is so strange, whoever can they be, why I didn't turn and run at that point I will never know.

I can hear myself breathing, I hold my breath and listen intently, no sounds at all, no wildlife, even the ocean is silent, something is moving, rustling, far at the back of the lean-to, I sigh with relief as something small and furry runs across my feet. I only dropped my guard for a minute and relaxed for a second, then somewhere in the gloom I heard a new sound, I can hear sobbing, my nerves are on edge, where in heavens name is the sad sound coming from, I listen, someone, somewhere is crying pitifully, sobbing, pleading, how can that be possible, there is no one here but me, could they be out on the beach or perhaps up on the hill. Whilst I was so completely occupied by the tragic sounds, I didn't realise that, somewhere in the darkness, slowly and silently, figures shrouded in menace and blackness were slowly moving towards me, it was only when they came within a few feet of me, did I smell the sickening aroma, that swirled into my nostrils, and then in the dim light, I saw them, many of them, so close, so frightening. I turned to run and I could hear and feel their gasping breath on the back of my neck, they were chasing me, I tripped over and fell face down into the muddy earth, quickly I righted myself and made a frantic dash, as I reached the front door terrified, I dared to look behind me and there was nothing. Inside I could hear my heart beating threatening to burst through my chest. The last log burnt away to ashes and still I sat looking at the dying embers, not braving another visit outside to collect the wood. Fitfully I slept, often waking straining my ears to hear the sobbing sound. In the early hours, the witching hour the crying stopped, and then somewhere above my head, the drip, drip, drip started.

THE RETURN.

It is a perfect spring day, the moorland has burst into
life and there is a definite change in the countryside,
even the wildlife is emerging from their
overwintering. This morning I could see the grey
seals hunting just a few yards out from the beach. The
vegetable patch is actually growing despite the
presence of just about every pest on the island
gorging on the new shoots. Betty came to visit
yesterday afternoon and said that she had read the
journal and wondered how I knew it belonged to the
lost girl as there was nothing to say it was hers, she
felt it was just a notebook left up in the loft, sometime
ago, most probably by someone who rented the croft,
after all people left stuff behind all the time, and she
knew because it was always her and Tom's job to
clear the place up, ready for the next rental. I cannot
be bothered to argue with her, or to point out the
shackles in the loft or the sightings. At the end of the
day, you cannot change anyone's views on a subject,

it is their opinion, we all see life differently. The only thing was, had Simon read it, I suspect not. I think he made himself perfectly clear on the matter.

This morning I had an early morning last walk on the beach, something that I will miss so much, I filled my pockets with more shells and little pieces of green sea glass, I might get time one day to make them into some sort of jewellery. I was hesitant as to whether I would be alone, luckily things seemed perfectly normal, I kept looking up high on the rocks, nothing.

The camper van is packed, I am not sure why there seems to be so many more boxes and bags, than when I arrived. The builders are still busy in the loft and have told me they intend to start on the inside of the croft as soon as they have made the roof sound and I'm out of the way. They assure me I will never recognise it when I come back, there they go again, saying when I come back. I ask them what makes them think that, they replied because the boss said, they needed to get on with it as I was only going to London for a while, so strange.

I am ready to leave, I have a last glance around the place, it looks as though I have never been here, everything is in its place, the builders are tapping in the loft, the same sound that has haunted me, throughout my stay here. I lock the door and put the key under a stone, the builders are sitting on the wall, having a lunch break, so, who is making the tapping sound.

I climb into the van, the builders shout, 'See you soon, have a good journey.' I wave and toot the hooter, half of me is thinking I have been too hasty, and the other half is saying, go back, you will soon know what you want.

I drive past the farm shop and luckily Betty is no-where to be seen. I am a little apprehensive on returning to London, as I still remember the reason why I left, hopefully time has made the gap between then and now a little wider. I intend to be back on the mainland by nightfall and then, I hope the roads will be reasonably quiet at that time of the night, and I can then drive for about seven hours and stop off in the village of Masham in the Yorkshire Dales for a few days, using a bed and breakfast I booked on the internet.

I drive through the small village and decide to stop for a few provisions to keep me going through out my long journey. I fill the basket with milk, biscuits, cake, apples and bananas, I wait patiently, there are two people in front of me in the queue. When the shopkeeper sees me, she pushes the other two aside and said, 'I expect you're in a hurry, I hear you have a ferry to catch.' I move forward and put my basket on the counter. 'It's a shame your leaving, but you are not the first, that place is bad news, always been something wrong with it,' the two ladies in the queue nod their heads in agreement. 'When I was a child, we used to dare each other to go inside, that was when it was derelict and the door was laying in the garden along with all the old furniture.' They all nodded, then the lady wearing an enormous Aran bobble hat piped in. 'Simon's mother eventually had it done up as a fisherman's rest, it was never very popular and I must admit we were a little surprised to hear you were going to live there. Any way you're off now,' and she added, 'It's for the best.' I knew at that moment I should have paid for my provisions, and walked away, but no, I couldn't possibly do that, could I, I just had to ask, 'I'd be interested to hear what you know about the place.' I waited for them to decide which one was going to tell me. The shop keeper decided she was going to be spokeswomen for the other two, she pulled herself up to her full height, looking as if she was used to having an audience, she gleefully unfolded the tale.

Apparently, the story was passed down by her grandfather, he used to tell his son, her father, many scary stories concerning the old croft being haunted, by the unrested spirits of a band of local smugglers, that used to wait for cargo ships to sail around the headland, and then they would lure them onto the rocks, looting the wreckage for tea, wine, spirits and lace, storing their illegal proceeds in the croft or the caves, before selling their contraband on the black market. She added, in a lower voice, the ghostly smugglers only appear when the weather is rough and the wind is blowing a hoolie. She was told as a child, the unrested spirits of the criminals were cursed by the relatives of the dead sailors, he deemed they were to roam the land for eternity and their families would never find any peace.

This all sounded familiar, my mind was taking in all the contents of the conversation, this was the first time I had heard the story and why hadn't anyone mentioned it to me before. I had to ask if ever a young girl was mentioned as haunting the place, they shook their heads and said, no, they had never heard anything about a girl, just the men, then they asked had I seen anything. I said it was an interesting place and it certainly had been an unusual stay. I added I had to go as I had quite a long journey in front of me. This place is full of surprises, at least I now know who the rowdy group of men are, though the girl is still a mystery.

I asked if they knew if any descendants of the smugglers still lived here, she thought for a moment and said, that as far as she knew there was only one person she could think of, and that was Jess, she had gone to school with her, but she was a little weird and her family had experienced a lot of bad luck over the years. I thanked the ladies, who seemed to have enjoyed the story telling and asked where Jess lived. With a map on the back of a paper bag I set off for Jackson's Farm.

I think I sort of know where the farm is, I have never been there before, but I have often passed the end of the driveway. I look at the car clock, I still had plenty of time before catching the ferry. I could never leave without talking to this lady that could be of help. I try to steer the camper around the perilously deep potholes in the uneven road to the farm, the hedges and ditches are overgrown and unkept and the lane gets narrower as tree branches protrude across the road. Eventually I drive through a gateway and I have arrived at the farm. I park the van and I can see a young man coming out of the cow shed, he doesn't notice me so I go to follow him inside the barn, but before I can say anything to him, he is back out again and talking to himself. I don't want to upset him, so I gently ask, 'Does Jess live here?' He stopped walking for just a second, and spoke quietly, 'I must go now, she's so hungry.' And he turned and went off the other way towards a row of empty stables.

The house looks absolutely dilapidated and in need of urgent repair, it was hard to believe anyone could possibly live here. I gently tap on the door and wait, nothing, I tap again, somewhere inside I can hear a chair scraping the floor and then footsteps coming towards the door. I am a little apprehensive as to whom I am going to meet. A frail lady answered the door, I can see she has used all her strength to open the heavy door.

At first, I am not sure of what to say, then I tell her I was in the local shop, and the lady who she went to school with said, she might be able to help me about the history regarding the smugglers that are supposed to haunt the island, especially the croft at Blakes Bay. She stood looking at me for a while and I think when she fully understood what I was saying, she stepped back and beckoned me in. She said to excuse her as she wasn't used to having visitors and wondered how she could help me. The interior of the house was really different from the outside, it was old fashioned but clean and well furnished. She asked me, if I would like tea, I followed her into her large warm kitchen, a kettle already sat on the aga and she instantly made the tea in an old brown teapot. I carried the tray into the cosy snug, she pointed for me to set it down on a table in front of the settee, she followed with a plate of fresh scones, a pot of cream and jam, which I recognised coming from the farm shop. I said I also shopped there and knew Betty and Tom quite well as I had lived at the croft in the bay. She said, she was pleased to have company and how did I get on with Simon Blake. I said as little as possible about him and that he had been my landlord but, I was leaving to go back to London.

Jess didn't flinch and listened intently as I poured out the story of my stay at the croft, I could tell she was going to be the first person who was actually going to listen to me, without making me feel as though I was going mad. I told her about the menacing men on the beach, the tapping in the loft and then I told her about my meetings with Alice Blake and my discovery in the loft of the journal. Not once did she interrupt or make a comment. I was like a running tap that no-one could turn off, as I was leaving the island, it didn't seem to matter whether she believed me or not, but when I stopped to draw breath, I could see she was interested in what I had to say. For a while she sat looking at me and then, she asked me about the notebook and what was in it, and where was it. I said I had left it with Simon, but I could remember most of it. I related most of the contents and then I saw a change come over her as I mentioned the stable boy, George, I then lost my train of thought and ran out of words to say, I was so sure she had something to tell me.

Jess pushed herself out of the chair and went to stand at the window, I waited for her to tell me what she was thinking about, when she turned around to face me, she looked weary, the lines in her face seemed deeper and her eyes were tired and had lost their colour. I thought whatever it was she wanted to reveal to me, was seriously important to her.

She came back to sit opposite me, I could see she was nervous, she held her hands tightly together on her lap. 'I'm afraid I don't know an Alice Blake, I might have heard about her when I was a child but, I cannot remember anything about her now.' She took a deep breath. 'I think I can most probably help you with the smugglers curse and perhaps the disappearance of a girl.' I sat back in the chair, relieved that somebody at last had listened to me.

'I have to be honest with you, my family has borne the curse given to my grandfather for years, and still we suffer from it, He didn't take it to his grave, it remained to punish my family. My father said his father suffered all his life from a series of terrible illnesses, mainly affecting his mind, and always said it was retribution for what he and his father had done when he was a young boy. When I was a small child, he used to tell us that he and his father had done a terrible thing, and that is why he had nothing but bad luck.' She stopped talking for a while as if she was deep in thought. 'Things were different in those days, people were really poor and would do anything to feed their family, it was hard when they saw the landowners living a good life, and they were working their fingers to the bone for nothing. Smuggling was an income, unless you were caught. When my grandfather who you know as, George, the stable boy, was an old man and on his death bed, he told his son, my father, that he needed to make peace with his maker as he didn't want to rot in hell, even the priest who was summoned to attend his last moments, got lost in the dark on the moors, and missed the dying man's last breath and confession of his crimes. When he died my father was going through his father's belongings and he found a faded letter. It was a long time before he felt able to open it.' Jess promptly stood up and I was a little surprised how quickly she moved. 'Somewhere here I have the letter.' She disappeared into a walk-in store cupboard, I could hear her rummaging around and things being moved about. Eventually she emerged clutching a yellowed piece of paper, she groaned as she sat down again. Reaching over she handed it to me. In the afternoon light I found it difficult to actually see any words on the paper. I asked if I could switch on the lamp on the table beside me. She smiled weakly and nodded.

'To whom it may concern, please forgive me for my sins, I have kept this secret to protect so many people. I was a young stable boy at Weathercote farm. We committed a terrible crime, my father threatened me that if I told anyone about it, I would suffer the same fate. I let my friend die a terrible death, I promised I would take her food, they stopped me. They made me lie to her family that I had seen her near the cliff edge. She was not the only one to die, my life is haunted by all the spirits of the sailors that drowned and my friend. They come to me at night and have cursed the whole of my family. Please God forgive me and stop the curse.'

I sat for a while looking at Jess. She smiled, 'I am so relieved to give you this letter, I hope somehow if this is out in the open, the curse will end. I said it was a shame that he never mentioned what happened to the girl after she died. I went to give her the letter back, she recoiled from my hand. 'Please take it, destroy it I never want to see it again. Over the years my family have suffered so much.'

I waited a while in case she wanted to enlighten me, then she peered out of the window, looking as if her eyes were watching something, far away out on the moors. 'Grandad had such a terrible drawn-out death, he suffered terribly, right from a young boy he was afflicted with one ailment after another, he was always out of work, no-one would employ him for long. His first wife died in childbirth, the child only lived for a year and was found dead in his cot. He then married my grandma, his second wife, she committed suicide when my father was a little boy. And the curse didn't stop there, my father was lost at sea presumed drowned, when his fishing boat sank off the rocks. The curse has lived on. I thought I might escape it and for a few years my life seemed to go quite well. And then I got married, he was a really good man and were so happy here on the farm, we worked hard to make a go of it, but so soon the bad omen started again. I couldn't give birth to a child that lived, and we had so many. My soul mate, Matthias, died suddenly, what seems a long time ago, I knew when he didn't come in for his lunch that something terrible had happened, all morning I had such an uncomfortable feeling. Even before I opened the barn door I knew, the whole farm was desperately silent, the hens that were always milling around the place, were nowhere to be seen, I found him dead in the barn. His death was unexplained and the coroner said it was a mystery. I knew different and so did others, others that knew about his father's crimes. None of this was my fault. You shouldn't have to pay for the sins of your fathers, should you?' She covered her face with her hands and sobbed, I felt so sad for her. I stayed a little longer and promised to visit her again sometime. As I was leaving, I mentioned that at least she had some help around the place with the boy. She said she didn't know what I meant, I said the boy that was here when I arrived, he went into the barn. She looked puzzled and said she didn't know who I was talking about, there was no boy here at all, I offered to look in the barn in case she had an unwelcome visitor, and yet I knew the boy was so agitated and possibly not of this world. She was still standing on the doorstep when I left the barn. I apologised and said I must have been mistaken.

 The day had flown past and the sun was setting over the hills, I realised that I would never make the ferry now, and the best thing I could do was get as near to the port before nightfall and then sleep in the van. I started the engine and as I pulled away, I saw Jess was at the window waving, my heart turned to stone as behind her stood a grotesque figure, Alice, and then I knew at that moment, I would not see Jess alive again. I think Alice also stalked and haunted the relatives of the men that had brought about her sad demise, including her friend George who, could never rest in peace.

COURAGE TO TURN AROUND.

The weather changed as I travelled across the island, so soon the dark clouds rumbled across the sky and I had to put my headlights on. I met hardly any traffic on the road, my mind was going over and over my afternoon with Jess. When I analysed the conversation, I had with her, I was a little nearer to knowing that Alice, definitely suffered at the hands of the smugglers, George, his father and others were responsible for her death. It didn't solve the problem of what they had done with her remains, I was pretty sure I knew that she starved to death in the loft, after she saw the men wrecking the ships, and storing the goods in the croft. What I needed to find out now was, what did they do with her body, I am convinced Alice wants to be found, so she can rest in peace.

I am so tired my mind is working overtime. I pull into the ferry carpark just as the heavens open and hailstones thunder down on the van. I feel like I'm in a car wash. Waves are splashing over the dock and I think it's going to be a rough night.

I have packed the van so high, that I have to climb over the seat to the back, and then unpack bags and boxes into the front seats before I can get to bed. Luckily, I bought food at the shop. I cosy up in the back of the van and listen to the wind howling and the rain beating on the roof.

I realise that with all that's been going on I haven't thought too much about Luca, it surprises me slightly. For the last two years he has never left my thoughts and today I feel guilty that I let him slip my mind, and actually forgot about him for a moment, how can that be. I know it doesn't mean I don't love him, because that love will follow me to my grave.

What an uncomfortable night I had sleeping in the van, it would have been a lot easier if I didn't have to share it with so many boxes and bags, and if the wind had just stopped rocking the van for one moment.

This morning the weather hasn't improved at all and if anything, the wind is a little stronger than yesterday. I battled over to the port terminal, to use the loos, and on the way back I checked on the ferry times. I am so annoyed, they have cancelled the crossings for the next twenty-four hours, owing to the strong winds which are apparently going to get worse as the day goes on. There is no way I am going to spend my day cooped up in this tin can. I use my phone to look up a bed and breakfast in the area, the recommendation is a guest house back in the village I have just come from, or a journey across the island to the western side. I start the engine, reverse and go back towards the village. The clouds are so grey and move fast over the hills. The roads are treacherous and every so often the rain is so hard that I have to slow down almost to a standstill. I feel the back of the van wobble slightly, as I skid on the muddy road, I pull into the side of the road and park, waiting for the deluge to cease, it was then that I caught something in my rear-view mirror, out of the corner of my eye, I could see there was someone sitting in the back of the van. My hand reached for the door handle and in a split second, I was out into the road, I ran far enough away to be at a safe distance, and then I turned, there was no-one there. The rain quickly soaked me through to my skin. I am not sure how long I was standing there, but it took all my courage to get back into the camper. I carefully checked the back seat, there was not an inch of space for anyone to sit, so what had I seen. I reached over the back seat, my hands searching for a towel to dry my hair, as I looked down at my hand, my fingers were clutching a frayed piece of faded blue fabric.

The weather was definitely not improving, and I certainly was not going to spend another night, cramped in the van. An hour later I pulled up outside the bed and breakfast, it didn't look like it was open, all the curtains were pulled together and downstairs the shutters were closed. I rang the bell and waited, nothing, I walked around to the side of the house, a large padlock secured a tall side gate. Back in the van I checked the opening times of the guest house, in small print, that I could hardly read it said, June to October. I suspected that the owners overwintered in their holiday home abroad. I looked up a pub about ten miles in the opposite direction, I phoned them just to make sure I didn't have another wasted journey, the landlord booked me in for six this evening, he assured me he had plenty of room and it came with full board so I wouldn't have to worry about eating. It seemed like I was driving on the moon, the beautiful scenery had gone and was replaced by a terrain made up of dark ugly rocks and small patches of dead heather and bracken. The sea was never out of sight always to the right of me, I was driving along a coastal road with a huge drop beside me, on a nice day it would have been spectacular but, not today. I switched the windscreen wipers to full and still had trouble seeing through the torrential rain. A sign loomed out of the gloom with an arrow pointing to the 'Ship' public house, I took a right turning and travelled down a steep hill until I arrived at a white painted stone building, perched on the edge of the estuary.

As I opened the door the warmth from a roaring log fire nearly knocked me over. I was greeted by a really cheery man, who poured me a welcoming cup of coffee. He said if I was hungry, he could make me a sandwich, if not it was only an hour to supper time and his wife was cooking local roast lamb and fresh vegetables, to be followed by her prize-winning hedgerow crumble, and of course real custard or cream if I preferred. He showed me to a small but cosy room on the ground floor, the side window overlooked the muddy estuary, the furnishings were really old fashioned but this added to the feeling of complete security, I remembered my mother having floral curtains with matching bedding, and pretty table lamp shades to match.

I returned to the camper to sort out a few things I needed for my stay; I was relieved the camper was clear of anything untoward. The pub is so cosy and nestles nicely into the rocks, just a few steps down and you are on a muddy sandbank, a lot different from the beach at Blakes Bay. The sky is so wild and angry, sending down heavy sheets of stinging rain that combines with the gale force wind making being outside treacherous. Just as I get back into my cosy little room, and switch the tv on, I notice my phone has three unread messages, Rob is saying phone me when you get this message, another is Simon saying much the same, and the other is the booking office for the ferry asking me to contact them immediately. I wonder who gave Simon my number. It is not long before I understand why they are phoning. The television in my room has an interruption in its broadcast, a banner across the screen says Breaking News, they show you the tossing and crashing sea, a cameraman and reporter are on the quayside braving the gale, the man reports, 'The ferry was sailing from the islands and capsized in the stormy seas, just a mile off the mainland, the air sea rescue and lifeboat, were out looking for survivors.' I should have been on that ferry, my name would be on the passenger list, but of course I missed it after spending too much time with Jess, perhaps a lucky escape after all. I tried to phone the ferry company, but the lines were all engaged, I should have let them know that I had missed their sailing. I phoned Rob, he said he knew I would be alright, but Simon kept badgering him for my number, he hoped I didn't mind him giving it to him. He asked where I was, I told him that I was held up and missed the first ferry and then the second one was cancelled, and because of the weather I still hadn't left. He asked why I didn't come back to the croft, I said I was quite comfy staying at the 'Ship' public house on the other side of the island, I asked him to do me a favour and phone Simon for me as I had to try and let the ferry company know I was not on the boat. He agreed and I thought no more of it. Eventually I got through to a number that was written at the bottom of the tv screen, a very kind person took all my details and promised to pass them on the right authority. I was glued to the screen watching the pictures of the ferry on its side with the lifeboat crew rescuing people on board.

At five o'clock the landlady gently tapped the door and announced that my supper was ready and she'd set a table near the fire. The pub was quite busy and I wondered where all the people came from, as I'm sure I didn't pass one house on the way here.

The dinner was delicious, I was so full I had to give the pudding a miss. I was in no rush to leave this comfy spot and when the landlord brought me a pot of fresh coffee and chocolate mints I sat beside the fire and relaxed, I tried not to think too much about the ferry and concentrated on all the things that Jess had said.

I thanked, Morag for such a lovely meal and retired to my room. What with the warmth and a pleasantly full stomach as soon as my head hit the soft pillow I sank into a deep, restful sleep. It was well into the early hours that I was woken by something outside my window, quickly I jumped out of bed and peeped out, the wind was raging and branches from a tree outside the window were scraping against the glass. I found it hard to get back to sleep and checked my phone, which was just as well as I had a message from Simon. It read, 'All ferries are cancelled until further notice, please stay where you are, I am coming to see you in the morning.' Well, I am wide awake now, what in heavens name did he want., It was far too early in the morning for me to be up and about disturbing everyone, so I sat watching an old black and white movie, with the sound turned down. I was relieved when I heard, the clattering of plates as breakfast was being prepared. I was showered and dressed long before I heard Dan, tap on my door and announce breakfast was being served.

I ate yet another hearty meal, lucky I was only staying until the storms were over, if I stayed any longer, I would need bigger clothes.

It seemed quite busy in the pub, a few farmers came in for breakfast, also a man came in with a basket of freshly caught trout and then, the butcher with trays of fresh meat. Morag had already made a start in the kitchen, making pies and roasting joints for lunch. I quite liked the lifestyle, really busy but pleasantly sociable.

I pulled on my coat and braved the storm to check on the van, the rain was so heavy it was hard to see through the cascade. I collected a few more bits I needed and was just locking the door when I recognised the Range Rover crunching to a halt in the car park. I wondered if I could make a run for it, too late, Simon had seen me, he quickly ushered me by my elbow back inside the pub. Dan greeted Simon, it seemed they knew each other really well. We both took our dripping coats off and hung them up. Simon's long hair stuck to his face and I must have also looked like a drowned rat. He accepted a coffee from Dan, and I felt obliged to take him to my room and let him dry himself on my towels. At first, he said he was okay and then, Dan said, go on, you can't sit around like that, Morag shouted a greeting from the kitchen he put his head around the door and had a quick chat with her. He followed me into my room, I didn't feel as awkward with him, as when we were in his croft, I was on neutral ground, it made a lot of difference. I showed him to the bathroom and pointed to the towels. Minutes later he emerged looking a lot drier. Dan brought two coffees, so I presumed we were staying in my room. I sat on the bed, leaving the chair for Simon, he sipped his coffee and I waited for him to start talking. He commented on what a cosy room it was, him and his wife often used to come here for Sunday lunch, Morag and Dan had been close friends since he first met Rowen. This was the first time he had mentioned her name. He seemed to be far away in thought, I could relate to how he felt, I thought about all the things Luca and I had done together and now they were all just precious memories to be recalled to prove, they really did exist, and those happy times were real. I think for a moment we were both lost in our grief.

The weather still raged outside, the lights kept flickering on and off and Dan brought candles in case we were plunged into darkness, he said he had a generator which would keep the beer pumps going and he also had an ager, even though it was a bit slow, we would be able to eat.

He asked how Simon was, they got into a conversation about work, Simon explaining his next visit to Italy to promote his latest work. Listening I understood exactly what Simon did for a living, he was an art historian and renovator of ancient pieces which he also wrote about, lecturing on the subject in many countries, mainly Italy. The men stopped their conversation and Dan looked at me, obviously prompting Simon to explain who I was. I thought I would leave it to him to introduce me. Perhaps I was the lodger, who saw ghosts, or the nuisance tenant who never stopped complaining, or the completely mad women so consumed by grief that I had gone completely bonkers. I waited, casually he said, 'This is Alice, she's a friend of mine, and has been staying at the croft, I'm having it renovated at the moment, and Alice was returning to London, for a while, luckily she missed her ferry, the one that sank, so I've come to persuade her to come back to the farm with me. I was going to interrupt; I changed my mind. Dan smiled at me, a kind smile, that made me feel quite sad.

Whilst the men carried on talking about the pub trade and the farm shop, I thought carefully about returning to Blakes Bay, I have a lot of pride and am not used to swallowing it, besides I'm all packed up and I only have to wait for the weather to improve. Unfortunately, the weather forecast predicted that the storm would last another forty-eight hours and at the end of the summary, she added that all the island ferries had been cancelled until further notice.

Dan left and closed the door behind him, Simon asked me to consider returning to the farm with him, he said I could use the barn for as long as I wanted to and he would appreciate some help on the croft renovation. He also added perhaps we could start again as we had such a misunderstanding, when we first met. Part of me was rebelling against him and the other tired part was saying, 'Just give me a break, I've been on a long battle and I need to stop and reflect my next move.' Apparently, I said that out loud. Simon looked at me a little surprised, I apologised and said I didn't mean to say it, I was only thinking it. He laughed, and said at least I let him know how I really felt, no frills.

On a more serious note, he said he understood how difficult losing someone was, and still now, five years on he still felt lost and angry, but the grief was not so intense, more an acceptance. He said the person dying was the most horrendous thing you can ever witness, but far worse was the thought that you would never ever see them again, so final. I was glad he got up and went to look out of the window, as he couldn't see the warm tears running down my face.

With his back to me he added, when Rowen first died, he had tried living in Italy, had been on cruises to places that they had enjoyed, but everything was so different, and she wasn't there. And now, it is something he had learned to live with and was grateful for all the good times they shared. He turned around, I tried to look away, somehow or another he was across the room and I was enfolded in strong arms. I can't say I didn't enjoy the feeling of comfort, but all it did was make me sob even more. He did no more than hold me tight, and then he released me and apologised profusely. I think he was waiting for my reaction, there was none. He passed me a clean white handkerchief and I promptly blew my nose on it and offered it back to him, he laughed and refrained from my offer. This was a really awkward moment, without looking at me he said he thought he should go, but the offer of the barn, still stood, and then he was gone. I was so confused, I don't know how long I sat in the dim light, I heard his car leave the carpark and I think I felt a little sad. 'Too soon, too soon,' my head was saying, how wrong am I to enjoy the arms of another man, how disloyal to Luca, what had come over me, allowing an arrogant man like that to become so familiar.

I had supper in my room and watched a little on the television, not really taking much notice of it. My thoughts were all jumbled with Alice, Simon, the croft and now my emotions.

Another boring day had almost passed, and still the storm is raging, only occasionally easing before the next bluster. This morning I checked again with the ferry company, it was an automated message, which I dislike, I really wanted to talk to someone and get more details, other than, 'No Sailings today.' I am seriously thinking of going to visit Jess again, it would take up a little more of the long day.

This morning I had an e-mail from Jeff my solicitor, he informed me that he had made a little progress in the purchase of the croft, he had instructed Vittori's, to purchase it, and he asked did I realise there were actually three properties for sale, all owned by the parent company, Blake & son. I was absolutely baffled I had no idea, he went on to say that he had made enquiries through the grapevine, as to the reason that the properties were all coming up together, he was waiting for the reply. My mind was a little confused, apart from Jeff trying to drag me back into my past life, by mentioning Vittori's, now there was the mystery of Blake & Son, what was that all about.

Dan is a friendly man and brings me afternoon tea and says Simon had just phoned and invited us all for a meal at the farm this evening, apparently, he has left me a message on my phone. Dan said he would drive; he was pleased as it was their night off and it was always good to get away from the pub. I picked up my phone and sure enough there was a message. Just for a moment I felt a feeling of panic, everything was changing so quickly, I felt things were becoming out of my control, an uncomfortable feeling.

These days I seem to go from one worry to another, I am just going to go with the flow at the moment, as every time I deviate it all seems to go pear shaped.

I change my jeans for another crumpled pair and try to find a blouse that didn't look like I had slept in it. My stomach for some reason is turning somersaults, I don't really know Dan and Morag, they are still strangers to me. I suppose I know Simon, but do I, can I trust him, worry, worry.

What a waste of time it was to wash my hair and try to tame it, as soon as I stepped outside, every hair on my head stood on end, then the rain lashed down and I could feel each straightened curl winding itself up into a corkscrew.

I sat in the back of the car and let Morag chatter away, my mind was far ahead thinking about this evening. I answered many of her questions, after a while I found myself peering through the car window straining my eyes to see into the darkness, we passed the turning to Jessica's and I had the overwhelming feeling of wanting to stop and go to see if she was okay, I have a strange uncomfortable whispering voice far away at the back of my mind, suggesting all is not well with her and I feel quite desperate to see her again.

Morag never stopped chatting and went on to say how sad it was Rowen dying like she did, even now they all missed her so much, and what a horrible thing to happen, it just goes to show you never know what's around the corner, who would have believed that you could travel all that way and not know that you had a time bomb in your brain ready to go off at any time. They said she was most probably born with it and the altitude of the plane caused it to rupture. Poor Simon, they were off to Venice for a short break before he went off on tour lecturing.

We drove through the gates of Weathercote farm and past the shop and Tom and Betty's house. Dan parked really close to the door; I instantly remembered the flower pots I ran over the first time I came here; I just hope I can behave myself this evening. Betty, closely followed by the dog, opened the door and said she was doing the cooking for tonight as you couldn't trust Simon to boil an egg, she obviously knew Dan and Morag well and they talked about the last time they were there and how good the food was. Apparently, we are having her speciality of venison cooked with grapes and shallots steeped in a vintage claret, roasties cooked in goose fat and the first of the purple sprouting broccoli, Tom picked this morning. Whilst she took our coats, she recited the rest of the menu, adding that Adam was here, Simons publisher and he had asked for a chocolate and Cointreau, tipsy trifle, which he always had when he stayed over. Simon came to greet us, he shook Dan's hand and pecked Morag and me on both cheeks, he showed us into the cosy lounge, a log fire warmed the room and table lamps added to the ambience. A man which must have been Adam stood up as we entered the room and Simon introduced him to me, I shook hands and smiled, as soon as he spoke, I froze, it was so good to hear an Italian accent again. Simon made everyone at ease with light hearted conversation about all the things Betty has to do for him, and made us all laugh at his failed attempts to do the cooking. I started to relax and enjoy the evening. Adam was also entertaining and pointed out many humorous things that happened when Simon visits Italy and how everyone who comes to the seminars want his phone number, especially the ladies. He said one time he arrived with just his briefcase and no luggage, since then Betty had packed for him when he travels. Betty put her head around the door and said, 'Could I borrow Alice for a while, I need a bit of help in the kitchen.' I was out of the chair in seconds, I followed her into the spacious warm kitchen. 'I thought you might like to help me with dishing up, I am not a nimble as I used to be and as Tom will tell you a lot slower. It's a long time since he had guests so I'm a bit rusty.' She paused for a moment to put a handful of mint into the boiling peas. 'Also, I thought you might be a bit overwhelmed by Adam. He can be a bit of a lady's man, especially when he's had a few drinks.' I thanked her and asked what I could do to help, she asked if I could fill the coffee machine and put the cups and saucers on the tray. I did that and commented how lovely the house was and asked had Simon always lived here, she replied that it was the family home, Simon and his sister inherited the whole estate when their mother died, he stayed and ran the estate and his sister moved abroad and became a silent partner, until recently when she returned to live in England, divorced and broke. My ears pricked up when she mentioned the sister, I asked, 'What was she like.' 'Oh, we never got on even when she only visited for just a week, spoilt women, greedy, even now she wants Simon to sell off some of the properties, so she can have her share. He works really hard to keep the place going, mainly with the help of his income, I think that everything would crumble if it was left to her.' All this time she had been talking and juggling pots and pans like a professional chef. I could hear laughter coming from the sitting room, they all seemed to get on so well. Betty said the venison needed a little longer and whilst we were waiting would I like to see the rest of the house. I said I would if that was okay. We went up the long staircase and came to a large landing, Betty assured me that in the better weather you could see the entire bay through the tall window, that stretched from floor to ceiling. On this floor she showed me the bedrooms and bathrooms, all a little old fashioned but quite luxurious, up three more steps and there was a small box room and a lovely large attic room, again with large windows overlooking the bay. I thought of Alice, I strained my ears to hear her voice, nothing, not even a slight feeling of her presence, this was her house but she wasn't here, she must be still roaming the croft and the rocks. I loved the house and did think to myself if this came on the market, I would be so tempted. Despite the cold and the size of the house it felt warm and cosy. I thanked Betty for the tour, and followed her back down the stairs, she said she was fine in the kitchen now, and I should join the others. Simon looked up when I entered the room and asked if I thought dinner would be soon, before I could answer, Betty shouted that dinner was ready. We went into an extremely nice dining room, again with a roaring fire. Betty said they only use the room on special occasions and that was not that often. Simon said it was always good to entertain with friends. I sat next to Adam and opposite Simon. The starter was quite delicious and rather filling, the Shetland mussels were poached in a white wine and fennel sauce, an interesting combination. I refrained from the warm bread rolls, even though the smell was quite inviting.

There was a pleasant lull between courses and I could see Adam was eager to chat, 'I am sure we have met before,' he said, I looked at his face, to see if I might recognise him, 'That's a good chat up line,' said Dan laughing. 'I am sorry but I don't think I remember you at all,' I replied. 'Tell me what do you do in the way of work.' I thought here we go, am I going to tell him the truth or lie through my teeth, I smiled, 'Owing to the loss of my husband I am taking time out for a while, that's why I decided to move to the Shetlands.' I hoped that would be enough to satisfy his curiosity. No, that didn't work. 'I am sorry about that, what did you do before you came here.' 'I was an interior designer, working with my husband who had a property company. I still run the company, but I have put in a manager, with instructions to only contact me if it's an emergency.' I sat back and listened to the silence. Simon was the first to talk, 'I knew it, you are just the person I need to sort out the croft.' Dan chirped in, 'I have a feeling you couldn't afford to have Alice work for you, tell me Alice where did you live in London?' 'We have a town house between Bayswater and Kensington, I have leased it out at the moment.' 'Oh my, Alice are you looking for a new husband yet, I think I would like to be considered first.' 'Please excuse my friend Alice, he's an amorous Italian and doesn't know how to behave,' said Simon. I tried to bite my tongue but it wriggled loose, 'Luca was Italian and had the most amazing manners and respect for women.' 'Please accept my apologies, I drink far too much,' he slurred. I just nodded, as a reply.

Betty came with the second course, Simon went to help bring in the vegetables and two more bottles of wine, which Adam immediately refilled his glass with. I noticed he did not sip his wine but heartily drank it in two gulps.

The meal was amazing, but I had lost my appetite, which did not go un-noticed. I thought, when you have been lucky enough to have had the best, how can you better that. I looked at Adam, his eyes were now bloodshot, I suppose he could be no more than fifty but his lifestyle was definitely taking its toll. I thought of all the Italian men I knew; I cannot fault one of them till now.

Simon and Dan chatted away about their teenage years and Morag mentioned how she still missed Rowen, and how much fun they all had holidaying and how strange it was, without her.

Adam who had been quite quiet during the conversation, suddenly interrupted, staring straight at me he said, 'I think I know, who your husband was,' he hesitated for a moment, 'Luciano Vittori, the property tycoon. I remember the papers talking about the accident and his ashes going back to Calabria. I could only answer, 'Yes, you are right.' 'Wasn't there someone else in the car with him?' he added. I don't believe you can come all this way and someone knows about all the things, you've been trying to get away from. 'My mother was in the car, it was Christmas and they were hit head on by a drunk driver, who was only slightly injured.'

The meal had started to become uncomfortable and I could feel Simon's annoyance of his friend, I thought to divert the conversation. 'Tell me Simon about your latest book it sounds really interesting, Adam started to speak but Simon talked over him. His book was about Italian renaissance architecture in the sixteenth century, even though he had a love of all renaissance art and had completely fallen in love with Florence. I listened carefully, impressed by his passion.

Dessert arrived and even though it was an amazing concoction of chocolate and fresh cream I declined the offer.

Back in the cosy sitting room I made sure I sat in a single chair, for fear of sitting with Adam. He seemed to have disappeared and I presumed he had gone to bed. We all seemed more relaxed without his presence, we chatted about the croft I said I loved the setting and the surroundings, Morag mentioned that Simon had told her about a journal I had found in the loft and strange sightings of a girl that I believed was a long, lost ancestor of his. At first, I thought she was making a joke of it, and then she added that when they first bought the pub, she refused to stay there at night because of all the strange things that used to happen, and it only stopped when she had a priest visit and bless the house, even though it took quite a long time before the hauntings stopped. I gave her a brief outline of what had been happening, Simon sat listening, but didn't join in. I told her about the smugglers and the visit to Jess, Simon was then very interested about the stable boy's confession, He then asked many questions, he said he had heard about the smugglers and their descendants living on the island, but it all happened such a long time ago and sometimes over the years the story gets distorted until the truth remains in the past. I changed the subject for fear of ridicule when Adam staggered into the room, he plonked himself down in the middle of Dan and Morag, Simon poured him a coffee and offered us all a refill, the fire crackled and the flames danced, drawn up by the raging storm outside. Dan looked at his watch and said we ought to make a move as it was quite late and it didn't seem like the wind was getting any calmer. I thanked Simon for a really pleasant evening and Betty for such a lovely meal. I managed to dodge Adam who was kissing Morag's cheeks with great enthusiasm, Simon laughed as I squeezed out of the door in front of Dan, avoiding his friend's attention, I called, 'Goodnight.' from the driveway, Ghost also squeezed through and pushed himself against my leg, Simon called him over and over again but the dog was adamant that he was coming with me, eventually he had to drag the dog away and hold him tight by his collar until I got into the car.

On the journey back to the pub we chatted about the evening and Morag said what a drunk Adam had become and it was a wonder that he could still be a professional publisher, Dan said men like him always had a lot of clever people working for them, so you don't notice their inability to perform.

The drive seemed to go on forever, the headlights lit up the stark road ahead, winding through the hills. Dan suddenly slowed down, he said he could see blue lights ahead of us, we drove around a bend and it was apparent what was happening. Fire engines were careering up a lane, we stopped, allowing them to turn into the narrow drive, I realised the drive was Jessica's, I wanted to jump out and race up to the house, Dan stopped me, saying, let them get on with what they have to do, we don't want to get in their way, looking at the glow in the sky it was either the barn or house. The wind fed the flames and in a short time the sky was red, another appliance arrived followed by a police car. Dan asked if I knew who lived there, I said I knew Jess and hoped she was okay and I would visit her in the morning to see if I could help her in any way.

We were all quiet for the rest of the journey. I was pleased to climb into bed, the evening at the farm was completely blocked out by the fire at Jessica's. The vivid dreams returned and I woke often in a cold sweat, Luca was dominant, but not the kind man I married but a monster, who smiled and held my hand and then when I looked up into his face, he had changed into someone I didn't recognise, but terrified me.

When the light of the grey day finally swept across the night sky, I realised that the storm had slightly abated and the roaring wind had eased.

Dan brought in breakfast and said he had just listened to the local news on the radio and he had some sad news, the police were asking for any witnesses to come forward if they saw anything suspicious at Jackson's farm last night, as the house and barn caught fire killing a women occupant believed to be the sole resident. My mind was racing, I am sure I knew who was responsible, and they were not of this world. I suspected it wasn't the relatives of the drowned sailors that waged revenge, but Alice, she had delivered her final curse to the very last member of the family that had incarcerated her in the loft all those years ago It was about eleven when Simon phoned, he wanted to apologies for Adam's behaviour and hoped he hadn't upset me. I assured him I did not take offence and I realised it was the amount of alcohol he had consumed that made him so lively. He thanked me for being so understanding and said Adam had been awake half of the night with his head down the pan and the other half with screaming paranoia. He thought the odd episode was sparked off by our conversation about ghosts at dinner, Adam had developed a fixation about a horrible woman standing at the bottom of his bed, he said, her ghastly gnarled hands, gripped the bottom of the duvet and kept slowly pulling it off of him. In the morning he told Simon, it wasn't the copious amounts of alcohol that made him sick it was the putrid stench that lingered when the presence left the room, which was just before dawn. I was cautious in my reply, an asked how was he now, he said he had just gone back to bed. I thanked him again for dinner.

THE HEATH.

Well, I made it, after three days driving, sailing and sleeping in the van, I'm beginning to feel like a nomad. After hundreds of miles and monotonous concrete motorways, I quietly arrived in England, I can honestly say I did not feel any emotions at all when I eventually parked the van and put the key into the door of this lovely apartment. The company owns this place, it overlooks the heath and is far too big for one person. I feel like a fish out of water, this life is associated with Luca, a rich life, but now quite meaningless, if I can live in the van, then I can live anywhere. Riches help, but peace of mind and happiness is far more important, it's not what you have, or where you live, or trying to impress each other, its deeper than that, it's to be at peace with yourself, something money cannot buy, and only I have the power to make that happen, no-one else, it's up to me.

It was strange going shopping, no chats, no gossip, cold well spoken, quiet professional staff behind the counters of the indie shops, so many beautiful boutiques, delicatessens and artisan bakeries, such luxury how can I be pining for misshapen bread, muddy carrots, pure milk and local seasonal produce, some would say I was completely mad.

This morning I walked on the heath but there were so many people all exercising their dogs, mainly small, sweet pooches, beautifully coiffured, wearing doggy Burberry jackets, with collars to match, even their poo bags were designer, I strain my eyes to see a mongrel or at least a natural working canine with scruffy fur and full of the joys of being a dog.

This afternoon, I have papers to sign at the head office, I am thankful I only have to do this once a year. The only way I cope with visiting the building is by being quite detached from everyone, I always insist on meeting the accountants in the board room, as I cannot bare to see Luca's office with strangers sitting in his chair. I also need to chat to the purchasing manager, to see if he's managed to acquire the croft yet.

I travel on the tube, what a miserable journey, lucky it is only half an hour, it is hot and stuffy and people don't seem to care how close they stand next to you. I feel I'm supporting a man who is talking loudly into his phone whilst he leans back onto me. I move, he moves. How can so many people be travelling at this time of day. By the time I reach my destination I feel, I should have a shower and change my clothes.

The office building is some architects dream, it reaches to the sky, made of glass that reflects the passing clouds and gives you the illusion that it is semi-invisible. I walk into the foyer and am greeted by a new young face, I give her my name, expressionless she stabs a few buttons on her computer and assures me someone will be with me shortly, all so impersonal and cold, but efficient. I stand looking at the foyer, it could do with some colour, the décor is either silver, white or glass.

The lift comes down and Jonathan greets me with an enormous smile, he hugs me far too tight. In the lift he asks me about my visit to the Shetlands and asks what I thought of it. I told him I had fallen in love with it and hoped to buy the croft. Jonathan was one of Luca's oldest friends and they worked together for years before Luca bought the business.

We travelled together up in the lift to the boardroom, hardly drawing breath, there was so much to talk about. A tray of steaming coffee and pastries sat on the table, Jane, Luca's secretary came to say hello and we chatted for a while, it was so good to see everyone, but all I wanted to do was sign the papers and leave before I started to reminisce too much and give into the memories that I was keeping just under the surface.

Jonathan was kind and realised I was starting to become uncomfortable, with all the visits from the staff, they only meant well and were so kind. He closed the door and passed me a pen and the papers, I read them through and signed them. He said before I went, he had to apologies for not keeping in touch, but now he would like to, I said it was okay, I know some people find it difficult when someone dies. He then asked me out to dinner and suggested trying out a new Bistro in Hampstead, I laughed and said he must have known I lived there, he said he hoped I liked the apartment; he had chosen it for me, knowing I like green spaces. I accepted his offer and arranged to meet him at eight.

I did a little shopping in town and decided to catch a bus back to Hampstead, I thought the subway would be really busy at this time of day. The walk from the bus stop was delightful, the trees in the park were getting their first flush of fresh green leaves and a lot of care had been given to the flower beds, in a few weeks' time they will be a riot of colour. Many of the Victorian houses had window boxes and residents had taken a lot of trouble to plant them with spring bulbs. This area is absolutely beautiful, all the houses on one side of the road overlook the heath, I am so lucky to be living in one of those.

I answer a few e-mails and notice I have a missed call on my mobile, from Simon Blake, now what does he want, even though I am hundreds of miles away from him, he still makes me feel uncomfortable, I wonder what I have done wrong now. I really haven't got the time to call him as I need to get ready to meet Jonathan.

My escort arrives in an enormous people carrier, I am amazed how well he parked considering it takes up two car parking spaces. I cannot imagine how unfriendly and costly this is to cruise around London in, I take him to task about the pollution, when he wants to drive five minutes down the road to the bistro, I can see he is not amused when I make him walk.

He has booked a table; the proprietor appears to know him and calls him by his first name. We are shown to a nice table for two in an alcove beside a roaring fire. I peruse the menu and decide quite quickly, I choose crab crepe's and lemon sole meuniere and a spritzer. Jonathan thought I should choose something a little more exciting; I firmly tell him that I want something light and fish always is. He orders chicken liver pate, followed by beef stroganoff and a bottle of Bordeaux. It was all quite amiable, we chatted about the company and how things were going and then I asked about the property in Scotland, he said he thought he had mentioned it to me earlier, and then he apologised that it must have slipped his mind. But the croft I was interested in had been withdrawn from the sale and the other two lots were still available so he had purchased them both.

I looked at Jonathan in disbelief as he carried on chatting, oblivious of my disappointment, he talked about his position in the company and how he felt he was now equal to Luca in knowledge and thought he was in a position to have a lot more responsibility, and as I totally relied on him for all company affairs, he felt that I should make him a partner in the business. I must admit he was right about me relying on him with reference to the business, but he was paid a princely sum for the work he carried out and I know he has a lot of extra rewards that he thinks he is entitled to. I sit and listen and then I interrupt his egotistical reverie, I thank him for all his work and mention the rewards I know about and the ones he thinks I don't. I assure him I will never have a partner; Luca would always say partnerships in business could cause grown men to weep at some time or another. Before he could open his mouth for another long explanation about himself, I mentioned the croft and referred to the e-mail I sent him, plus our telephone conversation, I asked if he actually listened to what I requested. He replied that the company could soon shift the land and property, it wasn't a problem and it was most probably best to leave the buying and selling to him and not buy anything on a whim. Besides he added the croft was not a good company investment, I assured him it was for me to live in not for the company portfolio. I felt absolute frustration at Jonathan's attitude and behaviour. We decided to have coffee back at the flat, I took the walk as an opportunity to outline my position in the company and even though I truly valued his opinion, and his friendship to Luca and myself, there are times when I expect him to listen to what I am saying. Still full of righteous confidence he assured me that Luca would have expected him to look out for me. What could I say, he was most probably right.

At the flat he made the coffee and we sat watching the lights come on across the heath. He obviously thought about what I had said and I know how hard it was for him to apologise, to me but that is exactly what he did. He said he would approach the seller's agent and see if they could come to some agreement, I thanked him, he asked why I wanted to buy the croft, because when he read all the details of the property it sounded absolutely decrepit, and then he added, did I want to live there because I had met someone, as it had been over two years since I lost Luca and I was a very attractive woman. How could I tell him yes, I had met someone and she had been dead for over a hundred years. He then said he had really enjoyed himself this evening and perhaps we could do it again, I said, that would be fine, and he added, what about afternoon tea on the river, next

Sunday, I said that was a lovely idea, he said he would phone me with the details once he'd booked it.

Long after he had driven his gas guzzler away, I sat in the darkness watching the lights go off over the heath and thought about all the people living here in their little boxes, some married, some young and single, some old, waiting for their maker, all with minds full of happiness, sadness, love, hope, grief, beginnings and endings, all these emotions experienced at some time in their lives, sunshine and shadows.

I fell asleep instantly, dreaming that I was in bed at the croft, I could hear the sea gently moving the fine shingle and shells on the beach and smell the ozone on the wind, when I awoke in the early hours of the morning, I was so disappointed to be here in this flat.

The sun is gaining its power and it looks as though it is going to be a beautiful day. I hear all the traffic rushing down the high street at the end of my road, and am grateful I don't have to join the rat race, every morning the traffic rushes into town and each evening it comes back again, by the time some of the commuters arrive home is must be time for bed, only to start the race again in the morning.

Today I am catching a bus and visiting a local market, years ago it used to be packed with stalls selling individual handmade jewelry, clothes and amazing food also a flea market, where you never knew what you were going to buy, but always came home with your bags bursting at the seams. The journey is short and so quickly I am standing outside an emporium where Luca and I would shop for Italian ingredients for his cooking, he was a brilliant cook and all his meals were made with authentic ingredients, made just like his Mother and grandmother before him, I wish I had paid more attention, I just enjoyed eating, not realising it would not be forever. I wander around the market, nothing really catches my eye, there are some beautiful dresses and lovely scarves but all I have on my mind is warm jumpers and woolly socks, where has the

girlie Alice gone. I catch sight of myself in a mirror and am a little shocked at my reflection, my hair is long and the curls seem to have taken hold where as I used to visit the hairdressers at least once a week to have it calmed and tamed, my cheeks are blushed not with makeup but fresh air, wind and rain and my handbag definitely does not match my shoes, what have I become, Luca would be horrified by my appearance.

So quickly I become bored with the stalls and feel at a distance from all this, it's all in the past when I was a different person and now it's all just a memory. I decide to buy fresh olive bread, a cardboard pot of sundried tomatoes and garlic, and a wedge of Pecorino cheese, a little bit of Italy sits in my bag.

It is such a beautiful day that I decide to walk back to the flat, I take a short cut through a churchyard where a group of people are clearing the grass and weeds in the oldest part of the graveyard. They all look like senior citizens and chatter nonstop whilst they are working, gradually they are filling their wheelbarrows and moving along a row of graves, I say 'Good afternoon,' as I pass by, a small grey-haired lady stops what she's doing and smiles at me, as I keep walking, she calls to me, 'Excuse me, excuse me, I have something to tell you.' The group laugh and shout, 'Don't take any notice of her she means well, she's quite harmless.' She follows me and eventually catches up, she's holding onto my arm to stop me walking, 'I am sorry to stop you my dear, but I happen to have an extremely important message for you.' I smile at her and the others in the group laugh and one shouts, 'Here she goes again.' The lady looks up into my face and says, 'You do know she's waiting for you. Why did you leave her? You have to go back, she needs you.' I am absolutely shocked, 'What was that you said,' I ask. 'I am sorry dear, take no notice of me, I'm just a silly old lady.' She calmly walked back to the group, knelt down and carried on weeding where she had left off. I wonder did she really say that or did I imagine it, I walk back to the group, one of the men stood up and stretched when he saw me coming. 'Take no notice lass, she's my wife and suffers from dementia, I bring her here as she enjoys gardening so much. I expect she told you she had a message for you, that's what she usually tells people.' I thank him for telling me and walk off through the gateway that leads to the common, as I pass through the great concrete pillars, his wife calls to me, 'Goodbye Alice.'

I stride across the grass making for the other side of the vast heath, there are so many people about enjoying the spring sunshine, I feel quite detached from them, I am still wound up in my thoughts and have no wish for any more conversations that will give me more things to stress over, I just have the need to sort things out in my head so I can file them away, but all I keep managing to do is, keep getting more files out, until I am overwhelmed.

I am quite warm when I reach the alleyway to my road. The cutting is a tunnel of beech trees and it is pleasant walking in the dappled shade under a fresh green canopy. My phone vibrates in my pocket and I resist the temptation to see who's calling, I just want to savour this peaceful moment for a little longer, besides nothing can be that important anymore, I've already had the worst phone call I could ever have imagined, nothing can ever be more life-changing than that, anything else feels petty and trivial in comparison.

I go to put the key in my door and find it is slightly open, I step back wondering did I leave it like this, I rack my muddled brain to remember if I locked it. I cautiously step into the hallway and am instantly greeted by the smell of fresh coffee. I peer around the kitchen door, Jonathan smiles when he sees me and puts another cup under the machine, I am so surprised. 'I was just passing and I thought I would invite myself in for coffee but you weren't here, so I thought I would make myself at home and wait.' He handed me a cup, I asked how he got in, he laughed and said, 'Don't be daft, I've got keys to all the properties, haven't I?' I really did not agree with him letting himself into the flat. 'I hope you don't do this to all our customers,' I said, I was a little perturbed when he didn't answer.

He made himself at home and asked if he should order a takeaway, I couldn't think of a good excuse, he ordered an Indian meal and a bottle of wine to arrive in an hour. We talked for a while about nothing in particular and then he chatted about his ex-wife and how she was fleecing him for every penny he had. I had met her at Luca's funeral and thought she seemed a really pleasant person, she had worked for the company, but left when her and Jonathan split up.

I never did know what happened between them and I really did not want to. He rambled on about her not deserving anything because he was always the breadwinner. I could feel my hackles rising, what a selfish man he was and quite a chauvinist. He wandered into the sitting room and turned the television on, something I don't usually do in the daytime. The sound of a rugby match filled the apartment and I excused myself and fiddled around finding plates and glasses in the kitchen and laying the table. I was quite relieved when my phone rang, it was the lesser of two evils.

I was a little late answering it and I interrupted Simon leaving a message. He said he had tried to call and leave messages to say when Betty was at the croft, she found a few things I had left behind. He wondered whether I would be returning soon or should he post them to me. I couldn't for the life of me think of anything I was missing. He said there was an amethyst and peridot ring, left in the drawer and a diary. I hesitated before answering, I told him the ring was definitely not mine and was he sure the diary was, he said, there was no mistake the diary was mine as Betty said it was best, he did not read it. I could feel myself going hot from my toes to my head. I said I would most probably be back sometime in the autumn if my plans go okay. I asked about Adam he said, he had left in a bit of a drama, mainly because he thought someone was playing tricks on him, Simon then told me how they both fell out and he was off to Italy next week to try and pacify the man. I wondered did Simon take Adams concern about odd happenings as nonchalantly as he took mine

I asked how the croft was coming along. He said

that, it had been a bit of a nightmare, the builders had so many problems that they couldn't resolve, they left last week and had not returned his calls. I asked what sort of problems, apparently, they had spent days trying to fix the wet patch, the roof was now watertight and there was no apparent leak anywhere but, every night when they left the patch on the ceiling would be dry, and in the morning, it was back even bigger than before. Everyone was baffled, and now when he had last checked, there was a black mould creeping over the ceiling and walls. He added at the moment he had hired Rob to clear the garden of all the rubble and debris that the builders had left behind. I asked what he was going to do about the croft, he replied, nothing at the moment, as he was so busy and to put it right would cost a fortune. He then said he was not sure if he had told me, but his sister wanted her share of her inheritance so he had decided to sell off some of the properties. I waited with baited breath and then he said, he didn't really want to part with the croft while it was in such a bad state as he would get next to nothing for it, but he had sold some land and another farm building. Then he said if I did come back to stay, I couldn't possibly stay in the croft and I could use the new barn. I couldn't help but be disappointed. I hesitated for a moment and thought, what the hell, I said to him, what if I made you an offer for the croft, over and above its current value, I would purchase the croft, and garden with rights to use the beach, and then I could get it renovated to my liking. The phone line went dead and I wondered if he was still there, he said he was a little surprised by my offer and would have to give it some thought, and then he added, 'Ah, yes, I see it now, I forget you have a property company, and of course I suspect you have already purchased, the land and the barn, no wonder you made so many complaints about the place, that's a good ruse to get the place at a knockdown price, especially as you know how desperate I am to settle the estate with my sister. And did you think that all that rubbish you broadcast about it being haunted would stop anyone else buying it?' I was so taken aback I couldn't speak. Just as I was going to deny his accusations, Jonathan crept up behind me and loudly announced supper was ready and whoever I was talking to had to go as the food was getting cold.

I was so stressed by the conversation and even more when Simon left me with a parting stab, 'Oh so sorry to disturb your dinner, I didn't realise you have someone there, do apologies to your partner in crime.' I turned to face Jonathan, I really thought if something heavy and hard had been handy I would have flattened him. He stood in front of me grinning, when I didn't say anything, he shrugged his shoulders and said. 'What.' Like a naughty schoolboy.

Jonathan wanted to know who I had been talking to, I replied just a friend, he tried to push the matter and I ignored him and when he wouldn't shut up, I told him it was my ex- landlord, and I had left some things behind, and not to be so nosey. I then added. When you get into the office, I want you to cancel the purchase of the properties in the Shetlands. I watched his expression and warned him, 'Under, no circumstances ever mention this to me again or you will need another job.

I was absolutely enraged by the phone call and couldn't settle to enjoy the meal. Jonathan was driving me mad with his endless chatter about work and how I really did need looking after especially as I thought it was normal to want to live somewhere so remote, then he added, even the people at work thought I was mad leaving a good life here to live like a hermit. That was enough I had his coat in one hand and I managed to steer him to the door with the other, he complained he had not finished his meal. I returned to the kitchen and filled a takeaway container with leftovers and pushed it into his hand and slammed the door.

I washed up and put the crockery away. I looked out of the window, my mind was going over and over the conversation with Simon. I suppose I should have come clean with him in the beginning, I didn't because he was so off with me, I suppose I was devious, but not that clever. I am in perpetual limbo these days. I can't keep claiming my bad behaviour is because of grief, I wonder is this the Alice I am going to become now I am single. I should have been more professional with Simon about the croft and not keep fighting his arrogance.

I have arranged for the locks to be changed on the flat, I informed Serena the property manager at Vittori's to what I was doing but I did not tell her why, I think she most probably guessed, she genuinely seemed concerned, she said Jonathan had been acting as though he owned the company since Luca had died. Then asked me to confirm I had requested that she withdraw from the purchase of the properties in the Shetland, she said she thought I had fallen in love with the place and was really looking forward to visiting me over there, and was I going to renovate the old farm property. Then she mentioned that another property had been added to the sale. I was intrigued, I asked what property she said she didn't know and would I like her to find out. I said yes, she said she would get back to me and should she hold the withdrawal, I agreed.

BLAKE'S CROFT.

Betty was absolutely enraged when she overheard the conversation between Simon and Alice, she couldn't believe he could be so unkind and thoughtless. Simon came off the phone and turned to see his housekeeper standing in the doorway with her arms folded. He instantly knew he was in trouble. 'I can't believe you said the things you did, whatever came over you.' He turned back to his desk and pretended to do something on his computer, the wise housekeeper knew him like the back of her hand. She knew he was upset at having to part with some of the estate that had been owned by his family for centuries, land that wars were fought over between clans, blood had been shed in order to retain the earth beneath their feet and now through Sarah's zest for living, the land so carefully guarded by Simon was to be dispersed to the highest bidder, which happened to be Vittori investments. She knew to leave him alone when he was like this, give him a few days and she'd get him to talk about it. She watched him close up on the matter, but she could see it was getting to him and how he was becoming quiet and withdrawn just as he did when Rowena died.

Simon wasn't sure why he felt so uncomfortable about the sale, he couldn't help but think that somehow, he had been deceived by Alice in some way, why didn't she mention at dinner the last time she was here with Adam, that she had already bought the land and farm buildings, and that she wanted the croft as well. It wouldn't have been so bad but for the first time in years he had found that he quite liked Alice, she was wild and fiery and he thought that perhaps they could have become good friends, but like a lot of people he had met she was just trying to line her pockets.

Betty listened carefully when he explained his concerns to her, he told her that after the phone call to Alice he checked with his agent and the offer was made whilst she was still staying on the island, and yet she never said a word to him about it, and if Adam hadn't recognised who her husband was they would still be under the impression that she was a sad widow, coming to the island to find solitude to get over her husband's death, instead of a wealthy company owner trying to expand her portfolio. Betty listened to what he had to say and thought there was a possibility that Alice didn't know about the purchase, after all she did say that she left others to run it and tried not to get to involved. He told Betty that the company bought up properties as cheaply as possible, renovated them to a high standard and turned them into luxurious holiday homes for the rich and wealthy and before they knew it the whole place would become a bustling holiday resort. Betty thought he was exaggerating it out of context and thought the sale was not his only disappointment, she had heard him at the end of the conversation with Alice, ask who was there, and if she was not wrong, he was jealous.

The last thing that Simon wanted to do was make a long journey to the airport and then fly to Italy to try and appease his drunken publisher, he was beginning to wonder why he was doing all this, it was all starting to take its toll, since his wife's death he had tried to keep so busy, not giving himself time to think, it was the only way he knew how to cope with the immense grief and sadness that refused to go. He had nearly let his guard down with Alice, at first, he had kept her at the distance he knew he could cope with, and then foolishly he had relaxed and look what happened.

Betty watched him as she packed his bag for the journey, he seemed to have been spending more and more time in the library, and then this morning he had slammed the phone down with such force that she thought a picture had fallen off the wall and when she rushed into the room he had his head in his hands, and when she asked if everything was alright he said, Vittori's had withdrawn their offer, Betty stood for a moment and then said, 'Surely, you cannot be surprised, you can't talk to people like that, and still expect them to be nice. You will have to tell Sarah she can't have her money just yet. She watched him get up from his chair, he seemed to have aged considerably over the past few months and she was starting to become quite concerned, she knew he was not sleeping properly as she could see from her house that, the lights were on in the farm well into the early hours.

It was well after three a 'clock when he turned off the bedside lamp and tried to sleep, he knew he had a long journey the next day, so had tried to go to bed a bit earlier, he managed to drop off straight away, but then something woke him, at first he thought he must be dreaming that just outside of his room there were bare feet padding across the landing. He got out of bed and checked, nothing. and then when he was on the landing a door at the far end of the hallway that led up to the attic rooms noisily closed, and footsteps could be heard running up the small wooden staircase to the rooms above. He had cautiously opened the door and looked up the staircase, with that, Ghost who had been asleep downstairs in the kitchen started to bark alarmingly, he went down to the kitchen, the dog was staring at the locked door, Simon unlocked it and let the dog out into the night. In the darkness he could barely make out a faint figure standing at the gate. The dog stopped barking and started to wag his tail as if he knew the person and then, as the figure started to fade into the night, the happy dog calmy wandered back indoors and settled down into his bed. Simon listened carefully, the house was silent, he returned to bed and the house became quiet.

After such a troubled night Simon rose quite early, he sipped his coffee and prepared to leave for the long drive, just before he left, he checked his e-mails, mostly were rubbish but as he scrolled down, he noticed one from Adam, it read that the visit had to be cancelled as he had to attend a meeting of publishers in Germany and he would get back to him when he returned. He took the case out of the car and rang

Betty to say it was all off, she wasn't amused as it was so early in the morning. He remembered last night, the odd noises and the figure at the gate and thought he should have asked Betty whether she was walking yesterday evening, as that would account for Ghost knowing who it was. He didn't wait any longer and called the women back, she was even less amused than before, and told him he should get a firm grip on himself as he was starting to sound like Adam and Alice. He didn't take the advice kindly and instead of apologising for disturbing her at this early hour, he put the receiver down, cutting her off. The housekeeper was furious and slammed the porridge bowls down on the table, 'Steady on old gal,' said her husband, 'What's got you rifled this morning, did you sleep on the wrong side of the bed.' 'Oh, be quiet, its damn Simon, he's been on the phone this morning, twice already, I don't know what's going on with him, but he's not been acting normally, since that girl went home, he seems to be in a constant bad mood with everyone and everything. He seems to blame her for all his problems.' Tom hardly listened and carried on spooning the thick oats into his mouth, a breakfast he had eaten every single day of his life since he was born. His wife was in a strop and he knew from experience it was best to keep quiet and always agree with her whether she was right or wrong. He pulled back his chair quite noisily and was greeted with a scowl, even though it was early he thought he would start his routine of jobs and besides, it was a beautiful spring morning and should not be wasted.

Simon felt a little lost now his arrangements had been changed, he also saw how beautiful the morning was, as he and the dog walked down the drive he bumped into Tom, coming up. They both nodded to each other and exchanged words about the weather, it was only when they had passed each other that Tom called back to him, 'Oh by the way, Rob said he was away for a few days so he won't be at the croft until Monday.' Simon nodded and then as an afterthought said, 'Thanks.' The dog raced ahead of him and ran through a gap in the hedge, Simon climbed over the stile and followed the dog, walking across the moorland he could see the sea far ahead and the croft sheltered in the cove. As he got closer to the croft, he could see smoke spiralling from the chimney and was intrigued to why there was a fire burning, perhaps Rob had left it alight yesterday, even though he wasn't aware Rob had a key, as he was only asked to clear the garden. Ghost reached the croft first and started rushing around following the scent of something. Rob had done a good job and quite a large amount of the garden had been cleared, all that was left was an area where the builders had stacked the roof stone knocking the dry-stone wall over and a great pile of wood, sadly he could just see the remnants of Alice's runner bean sticks underneath all the rubble, surprisingly bright red bean flowers were blooming amongst the debri. Simon had a good look and decided as he had nothing scheduled for the next few days he might as well try to rebuild the wall himself. He carried on walking down to the beach and as the tide was far out, he walked along the sandy shingle. He loved this place; he was brought up here and his father and grandfather before him. When he married Rowen, she moved into the farm with him, his parents were elderly and needed help to keep the business running, his sister Sarah, had left home years before when she was eighteen, she couldn't wait to leave and rarely visited, now she was broke and going through a second divorce and couldn't bear the thought that her inheritance was tied up in the farm and had also accused Simon of purposely keeping it from her. He had thought that he could pay her off somehow, perhaps by selling a few of the properties that were no use to him, he had hoped someone would buy them and just keep them as they were, he hated the thought of them changing, as Betty had said you can't sell them with conditions, he had replied to her, 'I can.' He was pretty sure he could have a proviso of conditions attached to the sale. Wearily he turned and retraced his footsteps, after the last conversation with Sarah he knew how desperate she was and if he was not mistaken, she was about to arrive any minute, something he dreaded.

When Betty closed the shop and was walking up the drive to put the takings away, she was surprised to hear a car coming up behind her. She turned around and quickly stepped out of the way as the car roared past her up to the farm. If she was not wrong, the red flashy sportscar was being driven by Sarah, the worrying part was who was sitting beside her in the passenger seat. When the housekeeper arrived at the farm door she was greeted by the loud brash women. 'Why is the door locked and where is my brother.' Betty told her he had taken the dog for a walk and she had a key, and when she put the key in the lock it was swiftly taken by Sarah, when Betty protested the girl said Betty wouldn't be needing the key anymore, because as she owned half the farm, she was moving in, and a housekeeper wouldn't be needed anymore as she was personally going to run the place her way, and then added Simon can do what he likes, I've had good advice and this is quite legal, and by the way this is my fiancée, Bryn. Betty was so shocked and upset, she couldn't think of anything to say, she returned home and waited for Tom to finish work to tell him the bad news.

Simon had walked so far that he was almost returning in the dark., the sun was surely going to set before he reached the moorland. The long walk along the shoreline had certainly put everything going on in his head into perspective. He realised he was quite obsessive with the island and would have to try all within his power to keep the estate together. The evening sky changed from a golden glow into a blanket of grey, he reached the stile, Ghost jumped over and suddenly stopped when a figure stepped out of the darkness. The dog didn't bark as Sarah walked towards them, Simon knew exactly who it was, her cigarette lit up her face and he knew he wasn't mistaken; his sister was here.

Simon entered the kitchen and knew instantly something was wrong, usually he could smell his supper cooking as soon as he opened the door. He saw Betty's keys on the table, he picked them up. 'What are you doing here, and where is Betty?' 'Bryn and I are moving in for a while until you find my money, we haven't got anywhere to live at the moment so I thought all this is mine as well as yours.' She hesitated, waiting for her brother to reply. 'I asked you where Betty was, 'Oh, didn't I mention it, we can't afford her anymore, and besides all the time I'm here, I will run the house and look after things, and while we were waiting for you to get back, I helped myself to food from the shop, we have eaten already, but I'm sure you can find something, or perhaps Betty will let you share their supper.' He was exasperated, 'I pay Betty out of my own money and I personally finance the shop and just about everything else, in fact I am out of pocket living here, I subsidize the cost of running the farm and all the expenses.' 'Then all I can say is, it's time to sell and split what's left. I want my money, now, do you understand.' She was joined by Bryn, he never said a word, but smirked at Simon. After a long explanation about the sale falling through and suggesting Sarah and Bryn stay elsewhere, he was shocked, when next, she informed him that, she'd already had the whole estate valued and Bryn and her had already put part of it up for auction, as it looked as though Simon had been stalling the sale. He asked which properties, she said, both the plots he had tried to sell, plus the croft, total sum being, exactly her half, it would leave him the farm and surrounding land. He tried to object but she said the matter was closed, adding she had as much right as him to arrange the sale. As for moving out, she said, when she had her money she would go and would never be coming back. He retired to his library and poured a large whisky; he could hear his sister going through the rooms claiming items that she said were hers.

 Betty answered the knock on the door, it was a bit early for visitors, but she had a good idea, to whom it could be. She was a little surprised how Simon looked, and guessed he'd had a difficult weekend, he sat down at the large farmhouse table, she poured him a cup of tea. She sat patiently listening to him, as he told her all the new events concerning his sister. She knew there was never any love lost between them as there was such a difference in their personalities. After a moment's thought Betty said perhaps, he should phone Alice and see if she would reconsider her offer, especially as the croft was included in the auction, after all perhaps it was better to let someone you know own your land, other than a complete stranger, and she also added, she liked Alice and he should apologies to her. He sighed and said, he agreed he should apologies but the sale was in a months' time and Sarah had said there was going to be a lot of interest in it. Tom wandered through and nodded to Simon, 'I hear she's back, give her what she want's lad, and get her out of your hair, you'll not have any peace till you do.' 'Yes, your right Tom, it will be easier to let her get on with it, than try and fight her.' Betty agreed to be re-instated at the farm and said she had known Sarah since she was a small child and wasn't bothered by her behaviour.

Simon had no intention of going back to the house this morning, but he thought about what Betty had said, and perhaps he should contact Vittori's and see if they were interested in buying the property including the croft.

He waited impatiently, tapping his pen on the desk, the phone seemed to ring for ages before someone answered it. He didn't ask for Alice, but asked to be put through to the buying department. Very briefly he outlined the property he was selling. He told the man that things had changed and the properties were now increased to include a croft that he thought Mrs. Vittori was interested in. Jonathan sat at the end of the line listening to Simon, he said he would look at the file on the Shetland properties, he pretended he was reading notes, then he lied and said there was a complete stop on the purchases and a block to any communication and besides did Simon not get the message he had sent him to say that all interest had been withdrawn. Simon asked if Alice was in the building, the answer was no, she doesn't often come in, he asked if he could leave a message for her as it was quite important, Jonathan said he would make sure she got it. When Simon rang off, Jonathan ripped off the top page on the message pad and shredded it.

Betty watched Simon from the kitchen, twice he picked up the phone and put it down then he wandered into the yard and leant on the fence and used his mobile. At first it looked as though he had a wrong number and then she saw he was speaking to someone, and she hoped it was Alice.

Alice was walking a neighbours noisy dog, when her phone hummed to say there was a message, sadly her phone was on the worktop in the kitchen of her flat. She was enjoying the amazing temperature, the dog lived next door and as soon as her neighbours left for work the poor thing whined and barked, so she asked them if she could keep it company and exercise him as she was out walking every day. Today she was strolling on the heath, she couldn't help but think of the island and how it must be looking now spring was nearly over and summer was on the horizon. She had only seen it in the winter and even then, it was incredibly beautiful.

Simon decided that if he couldn't get in touch with Alice then it was meant, he found it hard to believe, that after all this time the whole estate was going to be divided up into lots. He could see why his sister wanted her money but if only there was another way. It was strange how just when he thought things were changing for the better, that in fact behind the scenes things were slowly falling apart.

Before he knew it, he was walking towards the croft, he paused for a while, he could see how Alice had fallen in love with the place, in fact he now knew the feeling of wanting to lead an isolated life, perhaps he should move into the croft whilst his sister and her lover were in his house.

The sunlight hit the sea and the ocean turned into liquid honey. He was surprised to see Rob's pickup truck, and Rob stoking a bonfire with all the broken rafters from the loft. In fact, Simon was actually pleased to have some male company.

Whilst the men were breaking up the wood and moving the stones for the wall, they didn't notice the girl standing in the shadows watching them, she saw her ancestor take off his coat and throw it on the wall. She moved a little closer, it was only when the dog saw her and ran towards her did the men stop what they were doing and watch the animals strange behaviour.

She knew they would never be able to see her, but they could help her to rest in peace.

Rob hit a long piece of wood with a sledge hammer it shattered, as he picked up the pieces, he noticed something scratched into the wood, 'Look at this,' he said to Simon, 'Someone has written their name in the wood.' Both men tried to make out the words. 'I think it looks like a name, yes, it says Alice, oh, do you think she carved her name while she was staying here,' Simon looked at it, it certainly, looked pretty old, he turned the wood to the light to get a better view, he read the words, Alice Blake, and underneath her name was a series of numbers, from one to twenty-two, then they stopped, his mind remembered what his lodger had told him, now was this real or an elaborate joke. He shrugged it off to Rob, but kept the lump of wood. The men worked tirelessly and their efforts were starting to have an effect on the garden. With all the wood cleared, and the fire blazing, they made a start on the rubble and stones, some were so heavy it took the two of them to lift them back up onto the wall, both of them were used to building walls as most of the fields on the island were edged by stone. The work was hard a bit like a jigsaw puzzle, finding where to put the right pieces. Underneath the last block there was a pile of rubble and sand, Simon said to leave the rest for another day. As they were leaving, he went back to pick up the piece of wood with the name on, as he bent down he noticed a piece of carpet wet and worn buried under the rubble, he wondered why the builders had left it there and where did they get it from, they really were unreliable, perhaps they took it from the croft, that wouldn't really surprise him.

Rob gave Simon a lift back to the farm, he hoped his sister wouldn't be there, but as he approached the front door, he could hear her voice giving Bryn a piece of her mind, as he put his hand on the door it was wrenched open and a very angry man pushed past him, moments later the red sports car sped down the dusty driveway. Simon was surprised when he entered the kitchen, Betty was making a pie and Sarah was as quiet as a mouse, cleaning potatoes, if he hadn't witnessed it himself, you would never have believed the instant change in his sisters' mood. He was a little wary of the atmosphere, 'I suppose you saw Bryn leave,' she asked her brother, he just nodded. 'Well, he had it coming to him,' she paused and studied the peeled potatoes. 'I can't believe, he only expected to help me spend my money,' she looked at Betty and said, 'didn't he.' The housekeeper carried on rolling out the pastry, but nodded her head in agreement. As Simon was leaving the strange atmosphere in the kitchen, he said, 'He can't spend what you haven't got, can he?' 'Oh, brother didn't I tell you, the auction is off,' Simon stopped in the doorway, before he could ask, she said, 'It's all over done and dusted, no thanks to you, the sales gone through, someone made an offer and I agreed, I'll have my money in a few weeks' time,' she paused for breath, enjoying every moment of her speech. 'I told you I'd sort it out and I have. If you want anything from the croft you better get it before the locks get changed.'

Simon went into his office and closed the door, he was exhausted with everything that was going on, he hated changes and recently there had been a lot of those. He wondered who the buyer was, they would certainly want a return on their money, so chances were there would be a lot of new buildings and people for the island, even though they still had a planning committee that treated all newcomers with a sympathetic ear, recently he had noticed they were leaning more to the side of progress and had made it known that expansion was good for the island, especially if it brought in new blood and more families.

FINDING ALICE.

Alice straightened her skirt and tucked her high heels under the desk, this morning she was ready to take back control of Vittori's. After nearly three years without Luca, she felt she could now enter his office and not crumble behind his desk, she stretched her hands out onto the polished oak and absorbed the cold surface that her husband had once rested his hands upon, and just for a moment she could feel him sitting there working tirelessly to make the company as successful as it was. She was grateful for all the staff that had stepped up and continued to keep the place going, but she felt before it lost the essence that Luca had created, it was time to make a few ground rules before they lost their good reputation.

Jonathan was late for the meeting, most of the senior staff had been there for half an hour, when he arrived looking quite dishevelled. Alice was a little surprised when he did not apologies for his tardiness, and before she could speak, he was out of his chair walking around the room talking on his mobile phone. She waited patiently, the rest of the staff kept looking at him, waiting for him to finish, suddenly he was gone from the room. Alice leapt out of her chair and called him back, he motioned to her to be quiet, she returned to the office. This is obviously what the staff have been referring to, his rash and unprofessional behaviour.

She had received quite a few phone calls from trusted members of staff about their concern for the company and Jonathan's detrimental practices, she felt now was the time to step in. She had spent many sleepless nights agonising about what procedure to take and after consulting the senior members she had decided to have a meeting with Jonathan to give him a chance to explain himself. Sadly, she had a feeling he had got himself into a bit of a mess financially and personally and this was reflecting in his conduct. She hoped for his sake it was something that could be sorted out with the right help, which she was going to offer to finance for him. Addictions were illnesses and had to be treated the same way.

Jonathan came back in to the office. Alice waited for an apology, there was none, he kept looking down at his phone and proceeded to text somebody. 'Jonathan, please can you leave your phone for just a moment, while we have our meeting,' Alice asked. He barely looked up from the phone, but replied, 'You don't know how important this is, just give me a moment.' He carried on texting. Alice hoped his call concerned work, but something told her it didn't.

The secretary said they should proceed with the meeting and felt that Jonathan would soon catch up. When Jonathan heard his name mentioned he put his phone down, each person there had something to say about the changes that had been made within the company and how they were not entirely happy with them, as it appeared the company was suffering. The accounts department had been reduced, by making two long serving staff members, redundant, and Jonathan had decided that he would oversee all financial decisions. Long standing customers had been given new contracts replacing the originals, increasing the rents and a few leasehold properties had been sold at short notice. Jonathan at this point decided to comment, he said, he was running the company and it was his business to what changes had been made and if they didn't like it, they could always work somewhere else. At this point Alice butted in,' Just a minute I think we are getting a little confused to who actually owns this company, I left a team of equally qualified members of staff to look after Vittori's, whilst I was away, members I thought I could trust.' She looked at Jonathan, 'What have you been doing, you assured me you would consult me on any changes.' With eyes blazing he turned on Alice and spat, 'You know nothing about this place, I've kept it running all this time without your help, whilst you were running around the Shetlands trying to find yourself a new husband, besides it wasn't Luca that made the company what it is, it was me.' He hesitated for a split second and added, 'And don't you forget it.' Alice could feel her heart pounding and her mouth dry out, she sipped a glass of water and tried to calm the storm rising inside her. 'Before you leave Jonathan, I want to ask you a question. About a month ago, Simon Blake called you and left a message for me, why didn't I receive that message.'

'I don't know what you are talking about.' 'Let me make this clear, I know he left a message about the croft and land.' 'Oh, that man, been telling tales has he, you put a stop to it remember, you changed your mind when the man got nasty with you, I was in your flat when it happened, so don't start blaming me in front of everyone. I've really had enough of you and your accusations.' 'No, he didn't tell me anything, I do have other friends on the island, Jonathan you knew I wanted that croft.' Alice couldn't believe the way the conversation was going. He stood up and with a smile he said 'Besides, I don't think it's in the interest of the company to purchase any properties in the Shetlands, especially as it's only for your personal use.' Alice was exhausted from listening to his rude and offensive behaviour, she had known him a long time and was sure he was suffering some sort of delusional dis-order, only this morning the accountant who she hired to oversee the company's financial position had told her of an attempt to transfer properties and a great sum of cash to a personal account of a name they did not recognise. She had hoped that this moment could have been avoided. She handed Jonathan an envelope, inside was a pre-paid course, with request to admit himself to an addiction clinic, also sadly a suspension from Vittori's until further notice. At this moment she doubted that he was in the right frame of mind to accept that he was suffering from the devastating side effects of, severe class A drug addiction, such an easy thing to become dependent on, only realising the damage when it becomes physically and financially destructive.

When Jonathan left, the envelope remained on her desk, she dismissed the staff from the meeting, thanking them for their honesty, she sat for a while still quite upset about the meeting, she wondered how Luca would have handled it. She honestly hoped that Jonathan would seriously think about the offer and for his own benefit take it, in a few days' time, when he had calmed down, she would go and visit him as a friend.

Simon sighed as he stood alone in the kitchen, he was savouring the sound of silence. At long last his sister had left and he seriously hoped you would never return. Sarah had just about worn the patience of each person in the household, including the dog who spent most of his time hiding under the table. Betty was due any minute and he couldn't wait to tell her the news. The sale had gone through without any hitches, he still had to clear a few things from the croft and this was on his list for today, Rob said he would meet him there so he could give a hand with lifting the heavy furniture, he had thought of leaving it to the new owners, but some of the things were family items and Betty said she would like them. He had no idea who the new owners were and didn't really want to know.

Betty cautiously opened the front door and stepped inside; Ghost excitedly greeted her with his tail wagging furiously, instantly she knew the girl had gone, the dog's tail had been between its legs since the unwelcome visitor had arrived. When she entered the kitchen, she knew by Simons face, that things had changed, he was actually smiling. He told her of his plans, and she surprised him by saying she had changed her mind about the furniture, and perhaps it was best to leave it there, so the place didn't look so empty. He agreed, but thought that was an odd thing for her to say, as only yesterday she had said she would like the tall dresser and bookcase. The housekeeper packed him a flask and sandwiches and said there was enough lunch for him and Rob.

The two men started work to clear the last mounds of rubbish that were stacked against the stone wall. They were totally oblivious that, partly hidden in the darkness of the log store, they had an observer, they didn't even notice the slight breeze blow across their faces, as Alice Blake moved silently between them and stood next to Simon. She was watching him dig a trench to bury all the loose rubble. Rob leant on his spade as Simon tugged at a piece of tarpaulin that was well buried deep in the muddy hole, he leant forward to help and between them they dislodged it, moments later it disintegrated and revealed fragments of an old carpet. No-one could have prepared them for the next shock, as Simon pulled the carpet open it came away in wet pieces to reveal bones, small bones and strands of hair. Both men stepped back when they investigated further and exposed a small skull nestled in the mud. Alice Blake watched from the shadows silently, as the men pulled up the buried piece of carpet from the earth that had encased her, undisturbed for a lifetime, she watched them unwrap her shroud, and then after a hundred years of aimlessly roaming the island waiting for justice, she saw herself for the first time, once a young inquisitive girl in a beautiful blue dress embroidered by her mother with white daisies on, now a bundle of bones with fragments of her long blonde hair splayed amongst the mud, no one should see themselves that way. All the years of unrest of never growing up, of watching her parent's funeral, of seeing people's lives changing and knowing she was locked in this strange place, waiting to find peace. When the girl came, she knew she could see her and when the journal and the manacles were found she knew it was only a matter of time before her body was discovered.

Simon knelt down and carefully put back the damp rotten carpet, he knew instantly what he had found, the bones were small and entangled with strands of hair, small leather shoes had survived time and still covered the tiny feet. Rob moved away and stared at his friend in disbelief, Simon reached for his phone and called the only policeman on the island, to report his find of human remains. His mind worked overtime to remember all that Alice had told him about his ancestor being murdered and haunting the place, could this be possibly true, perhaps he should have listened to her.

Alice could sense that she was leaving this place that had held her secret for so long. She started to slightly fade, but not before Simon saw her ghostly figure standing at the back of the orchard watching them.

It seemed hours before the police arrived and then they said it was a job for the forensic team and not to disturb the grave any further, just in case it was a crime scene, even though he said it looks as though it was historic. Rob and Simon were grateful when he said that a local coroner was going to join him later and they were free to go.

When Simon returned to the farm, Betty was really interested in his find and said thank goodness as the poor girl could now be laid to rest, up in the churchyard where her memorial was.

The next morning the police arrived with a man from the coroner's office and arranged for the remains to be taken to the mainland for identification. Simon told them as much as he knew about her disappearance and said he knew someone who could most probably tell them a lot more. He gave them Alice's number.

Alice was driving with her phone switched off. She had set off after visiting Jonathan in the clinic, he seemed a lot better and had apologised profusely for his behaviour and agreed to take six months paid leave whilst he was in rehabilitation. She had felt sad and sorry for him, she thought this is what Luca would have done for his friend and colleague. Luca had been so much in her mind throughout all of the last few difficult months, and she felt somehow, he had guided her to do the right thing. Whenever she was in doubt or troubled, she would ask him what to do and after a while the answer would come into her head. She turned off the road and made for the bed and breakfast she had booked for the next few nights. Just before dusk the van pulled into the carpark, Alice was pleasantly surprised to see Dan waiting for her, they hugged and Morag came out to greet her. Dan helped with her overnight bags and took them straight into her room. She checked her phone and realised she had missed quite a few calls, she decided to answer them after chatting with Morag and Dan.

It felt good to be back on the island and she was happy to leave London behind, the company was back on track and not in the hands of any one person, but a group of really talented people she could trust.

Morag sat beside Alice and didn't stop talking about Simon and what had been happening at the croft, she said he had phoned her a few days ago and had been besieged by the press and a television company, because finding a body on the island was really big news. The blood in her veins ran cold as she asked Morag to repeat what she had just said. 'It's the girl, Alice Blake, the one you talked about being left to die in the loft, Simon and Rob found her remains when they were clearing the garden and I'm not sure if you knew the croft has been sold, so that Sarah, Simon's sister could have her money.' She stopped rambling for a moment as she could see Alice was becoming confused by all the events that had happened. Alice said she had missed a few calls from Simon and fully intended to talk to him now she had arrived back on the island, most probably tomorrow if he was around. Dan said phone him now, I know he would like to hear from you, he's had a very trying time, which I'm sure he'll tell you all about.

The three enjoyed dinner together, Alice gave them a brief outline of all the business problems that had stopped her returning sooner, she felt her eyelids becoming heavy and couldn't stop thinking of stretching out in a soft bed. She retired early to her room, exhausted by the extremely long journey, she knew in a few days' time, she would relax and the spirit of the island would take over and she would be back where she wanted to be, somewhere she felt she belonged.

Simon was pleased to hear Alice had returned to the island and was staying with Morag, he was sure she already knew about his discovery and the croft being sold. This morning she had phoned and he wasn't sure why he felt so jittery about meeting her again, he could only think that it was because of their last conversation, when she was in London and he accused her of malpractice, he knew, he still owed her an apology. Betty grinned to herself when he informed her that Alice was back on the island and was coming to lunch, she could see he was not his usual calm self, before she left for the shop, she put two ploughman's lunches in the fridge and said there were fresh rolls in the bread bin, and not to forget to make a pot of coffee.

Alice enjoyed the journey through the green hills, again the whole landscape had changed and the colours of summer were vibrant, above the hills the sky was azure blue and not a single cloud interrupted the vast expanse. As if by magic she turned a corner and the countryside changed, she wound her way through moorland speckled with sheep grazing on the luscious grass, but the most moving sight of all, was when she drove around a rocky crag protruding into the road, she gasped with delight, there in front of her was the sight she had often dreamt about, the ocean stretched out into the distance, she could feel it under her feet and smell the ozone and suddenly she felt at peace. Driving down the lane to Blakes Bay, tears filled her eyes and just for a moment she thought she heard Luca's voice, he said. 'This is lovely, you'll be alright here,' and then he was gone, and something inside her felt him leaving and she knew it was time for her to let him rest in peace, and not keep him alive in her mind, waiting for him to come back.

As she approached the bay, she couldn't help but look high up on the rocks, she wasn't sure, that now Alice had been found, would her ghost still haunt the place, so quickly her question was answered, as she slowed down to turn off into the small layby outside the croft, to park, a figure stood in the orchard barely hidden by the trees that were in full leaf. Even though she had eventually got used to having the ghost appear without warning, she would rather the spirit moved on.

Stepping out of the van, she could see the blue and white tape around the newly discovered grave, the exact place where she had planted the runner beans. She approached Alice, and could instantly see that she had completely changed, she was a young and beautiful girl, gone was the haggard skeleton with decaying flesh hanging in shreds with a haunting plea in her faded blue eyes, a sight etched into her brain never to be forgotten, The beautiful girl in front of her was smiling, wearing her blue dress, which was crisp and new, Alice Blake silently glided towards her and stretched out a long slim hand and gently touched Alice's face, on her finger she wore a peridot and amethyst ring, for a moment they both stood locked in time. Alice closed her eyes and saw all that had gone before, playing in her mind like a vivid movie, thoughts and emotions passed between the two, like a bolt of lightning, and as painful as it was, when they parted, both had changed and learnt so much.

When Alice opened her eyes, she was on her own and as she turned to walk away, a white feather floated down slowly in front of her, she reached out and it landed softly in her hand, what a treasure, she knew at that moment things were quite different, she didn't feel locked in immense grief anymore and though her life had been sad after her loss, something reminded her you only die once, but you get to live many days and they are the ones to use wisely and cherish while they last.

She walked up to the front door and picked up a flower pot, and there was the large iron key, just where her agent had asked Simon to leave it. She entered the cottage and was pleased to see the damp patch on the ceiling had completely dried up and most things were virtually the same as she had left them. For now, she would keep the place as it was and then gradually over time make a few changes here and there to make it more comfortable.

Simon waited patiently at the farm, he kept straining his ears to hear the camper van arrive, she was quite late, his phone rang and it was Alice, she asked him to meet her at the croft, he mentioned that the croft wasn't his anymore as it had been sold, she said she knew.

He hadn't expected to have to drive to the croft again. Alice was waiting at the door, before he got out of the car a strange thought came into his head and when she opened the door and invited him in, he knew his suspicion was correct. He was quite relieved she was the new owner, knowing her love of the island, he couldn't see her filling the place with holidaymakers.

Simon kissed Alice on both cheeks and said how good it was to see her again, he started to apologies for his bad manners regarding the phone call, she laughed and told him not to worry, a lot had happened since then and she had completely forgotten about it. He asked if she was the person that put in an offer before the auction, she said she had to come clean, yes it was, but she wouldn't have known about it without the help of Betty who phoned her as soon as his sister had said she had arranged for it all to go to auction.

Alice thought Simon had changed a little since she had last seen him, he had grey streaks at the sides, peppering his long chestnut hair, happily she also noticed he was genuinely pleased about her purchasing the properties. He said there was so much to tell her about finding Alice Blakes remains, and suggested they go back to the farm for lunch as Betty had prepared one of her special Ploughman's. She said that was a good idea, but first would he like to be useful, and help her unpack the camper.

When the camper was quite empty and the croft was brimming from floor to ceiling with boxes of all shapes and sizes, Alice relaxed, and said she had worked up an appetite and was looking forward to Betty's food, something that she had really missed. He offered to give her a lift, refusing she said she would follow him up to the farm as she wasn't staying at the croft tonight as she was going back to the pub for a few days until she had aired the place and bought supplies.

Betty smiled and waved, frantically as she drove past the shop. Simon opened the front door, and before Alice could step inside Ghost launched himself at Alice from the kitchen, he howled and turned circles, chased his tail and stood in front of her until she stroked him until her arm ached.

It was good to see the farm in summer, with all the windows open and the sun beaming in, the whole place looked and felt so much lighter.

Outside the kitchen door was a pretty courtyard with a long wooden table and odd chairs, that overlooked the rolling green fields, Alice and the dog sat at the table watching brown hares rushing through the long grass, Simon appeared from the kitchen with two plates and went back in to make the coffee, whilst he waited for the machine to splutter, he found the things that he wanted to give Alice. Alice entered the kitchen and offered her help and asked where the cutlery was kept. He motioned to a drawer in the long pine table, Alice selected the cutlery and helped herself to napkins, Simon said the bits in the box were for her, but it didn't matter if she didn't want them. She was curious to the piece of wood sticking out of the box, without warning she was filled with overwhelming sadness as she read the name and saw the number of days the girl had crossed off while slowly dying in the loft. The journal, locket and ring were also in the box, he said he thought she should have the ring as he was sure it was something to do with Alice Blake, she thanked Simon, saying she would treasure them and take them back to the croft as she felt they belonged there. She asked what would happen to Alice's remains, he said he thought it would be fitting to have her placed beneath her memorial stone, not so much a funeral but a respectful internment, and perhaps she would like to join him, Alice said that sounded a good idea and she would be pleased to be there.

Lunch was quite drawn out; Alice was pleased that they both seemed more relaxed in each other's company. She suddenly remembered Adam and asked how he was, Simon confessed that he had been a bit hasty with him and at the end of the month he was going out to Italy to make peace, and discuss his next publication, in fact, he had quite an itinerary, visiting Florence, a lecture in Venice, and then a couple of weeks recuperating taking in the sights and catching up with friends. Alice listened to his plans and quite envied him, she said it sounded amazing and Italy was certainly a place to spend time in, she talked about the region that Luca had come from and that she'd had many happy holidays, picking olives and oranges from his family's Groves, well more like fields. He wondered if she was still in touch with them, she said that most of them were very old or dead, and she hadn't visited them since she returned Luca's ashes to the family vault.

With lunch over, Alice forced Simon to wash up the dishes instead of leaving them for Betty, he disapproved and had no idea on how to begin, after a jovial lesson on cleaning dishes it was decided that they should take Ghost for a walk, the day was so beautiful it was a shame to waste it. The dog bounded off over the stile and raced off across the field in the direction of the hares, Simon assured Alice that the dog wouldn't touch the creatures as he hated anything furry in his mouth, in fact he was a failed gundog and that is how they had come by him. Alice raced ahead eager to see the ocean, something she had thought about so much, she laughed as she looked down on her croft, it looked like a miniature cottage, Simon caught up with her and they both stopped to look at the most amazing view.

The summer gave the countryside a depth and colourful glow, which wasn't there in the winter. The dog seemed to know exactly where they were going, and when they reached the ruins instead of walking past, he disappeared through a thicket of untidy trees, Alice commented that she couldn't see where Ghost had gone, 'Ah,' said Simon, 'Just you wait and see, it's one of his favourite walks, he used to do it daily with his mistress. If you're ready for a long walk we could follow him, but if you're in a hurry to get back, don't worry.' Alice assured him she was in no rush and to see a new part of the island was really exciting. They squeezed their way through the bushes and before them was a narrow pathway, leading downwards, nettles and wildflowers had grown over the unused path, she asked why it was so overgrown, if it was one of his popular walks, he said it was well used when his wife was alive and they would walk it often, since she had died, it was not the same, he led the way through the tall Fireweed that moved in the slight breeze, some was nearly as tall as Alice. Bees buzzed busily around the tall pink plants and the grasses were abundant a host to colourful beetles and moths. Alice could feel the heat of the sun beating down on her back and bites around her ankles where disturbed insects fed off her hot skin. Simon marched on, occasionally looking around to make sure she was still there, all she could think about as they continued on downwards was the climb back up again, facing the scorching sun.

The path opened out into a large clearing and ahead Alice could see a most unusual sight, a copse of tall trees, which was a welcoming sight after such a long exposer to the sweltering sunshine. What a welcome relief when they entered the pocket of wilderness, it was quite a magical sight, suddenly it was dark and cool, the canopy of the trees was so thick no sun could penetrate the density of the fresh green leaves. Bright green ferns and beautiful white flowered woodruff formed a carpet, in the shade mosses coated rocks and fallen branches, the earth was soft and spongy, in front of them the dog had found a small trickling stream and was drinking heartily, Alice trailed her hands through the cool water, mosses and ferns had overspilled and gently edged the snaking stream. Simon watched Alice as she peeled off her shoes and walked through the cool water, years ago he had seen someone else do that, Alice was like a child paddling in the sea, the dog joined her and soon they both became wetter and wetter. 'I love this place Simon, who would have known it was here, I have walked past the entrance a dozen times and never noticed it.' He smiled and said he had something else to show her, she stepped out of the water and sunk her feet into the soft green moss, leaving her shoes on the bank she followed him, they crossed the stream and headed to a wall of rock, splattered here and there with ferns hanging from deep cracks and as Simon stood back she could see a small opening with water trickling down into a rock pool 'This is a Holy well, fed by a spring, the water is pure and good enough to drink, some say it has magical powers and others say the pilgrims used to worship here and others used to take the water for its healing properties, I think it contains various harmless natural ingredients.' He stopped talking and reached down to pick up a small bunch of white daisies that were tucked beside the well, he handed them to Alice, she knew who had placed them there, he watched her animated face as she drunk more from the crystal-clear water, and when she stopped drinking, he could see that she was really happy being in the small forest, it was such a rarity to find such trees on the island. Alice was so relaxed and happy and thanked him for bringing her here and said she would visit it often if he didn't mind, he laughed and said he didn't own it, but not many people knew it was there, so it was always a secret sanctuary.

The dog tired of foraging for small creatures he could chase flopped himself down at her feet, she sat down on a tree trunk that had fallen creating a green velvet seat, Simon sat beside her, they both watched the stream trickling past on its journey.

Simon talked about Rowen and how this was her favourite place and how long it took to come to grips with her leaving, and how sometimes when he wakes in the morning just for a moment, he has forgotten she has died. Alice said losing Luca was the worst thing that had ever happened to her, she had thought the raw pain would be with her forever and had wondered how she would ever be able to function normally again, especially when her head was so distant from everything and everyone. She said how gradually her grief had changed, the pain of loss was the same, but she had learnt to live alongside it, never really believing what had happened, eventually you evolve as a new person alone, shocked, and so extremely sad, its private to you and no-one can really help, it's your journey and there are no rules, you have to do it your way.

Simon put an arm around her, she tried not to give in to the tears that were so ready to fall, she was so tired of fighting the world and standing on her own. They sat for a long time in the magical woodland listening to the birds singing high up in the trees, they comforted each other in their grief and when the sun was setting and the dog became restless, they left hand in hand, in silence they walked back up the hill, they arrived back at the farm when the sun had nearly set casting long shadows over the island. She was reluctant to leave and go back to the pub and followed Simon into the garden, he brought out a bottle of wine and glasses, without words he poured the wine and stood beside her. 'I have been thinking and correct me if I am being too forward, but without any strings attached and purely as a travelling companion, would you like to join me on my trip, I think you would enjoy it as much as me. At least we would have something in common, our love of Italy.' He stopped quite abruptly and looked as though he immediately regretted what he had said. Alice didn't need too much time to think about it, she stood up and turned to him and on tip toe she reached up and gently kissed him, at first, he didn't respond and just when she felt it was a mistake, he put his strong arms around her and returned the kiss.

Morag was starting to get a little worried that Alice had not returned since that morning, as she remembered her saying that she would be back for supper. Morag wanted to phone Simon, to see if she was alright, Dan said, 'No, I think we should leave them well alone.'

Laddie was so pleased to see his mistress Alice, he jumped and squealed, turning circles he chased his tale.

'Come along Alice, we seem to have been waiting a lifetime for you to catch us up. We watched you roaming and making a nuisance of yourself, that poor girl. You are going to love it here; you can do anything you like, it's Heaven.' Said Alice Blake's Mother.

END OF STORY

Printed in Great Britain
by Amazon

57399014R00142